Swimming on Dry Land

For Slavek

Swimming on Dry Land

Helen Blackhurst

Seren is the book imprint of
Poetry Wales Press Ltd
57 Nolton Street, Bridgend, Wales, CF31 3AE
www.serenbooks.com
Facebook: facebook.com/SerenBooks
Twitter: @SerenBooks

ISBN: 978-1-78172-291-6

Typesetting by Elaine Sharples
Printed by CPI Group (UK) Ltd, Croydon

The publisher works with the financial assistance of
The Welsh Books Council

MONICA

The whole town is out looking for Georgie. She's been missing two days now. She is two rulers smaller than me, with curly mouse-brown hair and a crooked thumb on her left hand. Last seen, she was wearing my orange cardigan. When I say the whole town, I mean the women. It's a mining town. Most of the men are five miles away at the central site. Except Dad and Uncle Eddie. They're helping the detectives work out what to do next. Mum is in charge. She and her best friend, Maddie, are leading a group of women out the Wattle Creek road. She told me to stay in bed. The reason I am not in bed is because I don't feel ill. We should have stayed in England. Things like this only happen in Australia.

We moved here a year ago because Uncle Eddie said he'd help us out. Uncle Eddie is pretty good that way. I clean his house and he gives me pocket money, although there isn't much to spend it on. If we were at home, I'd be able to get books from Wogan's Bookshop – three for a pound. Mrs Wogan used to give me the really dirty ripped-around-the-edges ones for free. I miss Wogan's. There are nine books in my suitcase, but I've read them all at least ten times. I've read Dad's books too. When we go home, the first thing I'm going to do is bike down to Wogan's. Mrs Wogan probably won't recognise me. My skin is freckly brown now, and my hair is twice as long. Did you know that Georgie can't read? She only looks at the pictures.

The way it works in Akarula is that Dad helps Uncle Eddie, when he's feeling up to it, and Mum does just about everything else. I'm in charge of Georgie. That's why, whichever way you look at it, this is all my fault.

We are playing hide and seek the day Georgie disappears. It's the kind of game she likes. She is only four. I'm nearly twelve. She goes off to hide and I sit on the caravan steps and watch Dad feed the birds. He's like a statue, standing there behind Uncle Eddie's house, his stretched-out hand full of birdseed. Those Galahs must love him. They're beautiful: pink and grey, like old ladies' coats. I do a sketch of him and the birds in my notebook. Mum thinks Dad shouldn't feed the birds. She doesn't realise they would die without him. Dad is mad about wildlife. He likes birds and insects the most.

When I'm done, I shove my notebook in the back pocket of my pedal-pushers and head off to look for Georgie. The sun is scorching. I use my cap to shade my eyes. I'm getting used to the heat. In the first few weeks I could hardly move, but once you slow down and keep your head covered, it's not so bad. I look between the cars, the trucks and road trains parked up behind the pumps; most of them have Lansdowne Mining Corporation stamped on the side in green lettering. You'd want to see these road trains, great huge things. I wouldn't mind driving one some day.

Georgie usually hides in between the wheels. But I can't see her. She's not behind the oil barrels either, or the pile of old tyres thrown in the scrub on the edge of the tarmac. I search around the outside of Uncle Eddie's shed, which is padlocked, so she can't be inside. I'll kill her if she ruins my cardigan. It doesn't even fit her properly; the sleeves are way too long.

I climb Red Rock Mountain. It's not really a mountain, more like a big rock that sticks up behind the caravan. Dad calls it a mountain. Compared with the flat bush around, I suppose it is.

It's quite steep; halfway up you have to crawl and grab hold of the jutting ledges. Uncle Eddie has warned us to watch out for snakes. I keep my eyes peeled. Not been lucky yet though. I love snakes. I've got a book of snakes with all the Latin names and what they do and whether they are poisonous or not. There are seven families of snakes in Australia, about 140 species. The most deadly ones are brown snakes, copperheads, death adders, red-bellied black snakes, taipans, and tiger snakes. Those clumps of scrub grass dotted over the rock are good places for them to hide.

The last stretch is the hardest. It's really steep. You have to watch where you're putting your hands. Once I'm at the top, I make my way over to the highest rock. From up here you can see the whole town. The mine is pretty far off but the machines stick out in the cleared scrub. Then there's the water tank, and nearer still, Akarula town. It's not much of a town: a long red dirt road with one-storey houses on either side, a general store that sells everything – except books – and the bar. The road bends just after the tree at the end and loops round to our service station. You can't go farther than us. The road just stops. If you drive the other way, you'll eventually get to Adelaide, I think. Or somewhere. You have to pass through Wattle Creek, which is why everyone calls it the Wattle Creek road. Behind the street are the mobile homes and trailers; beyond them, hundreds of termite mounds sticking up like gravestones, spreading out into the bush. No sign of Georgie. Nothing moves, except the road trains and mining trucks, and the odd beaten-up car. There is no wind either. Sometimes when I'm walking, I feel as if I'm standing still.

I can see Mr M sitting underneath the white-barked tree. He can't see me though, which is a good thing. He doesn't like people climbing Red Rock Mountain in case they wake the

Rainbow Snake. I've never seen that snake and I've stamped and shouted really loud on this rock. Imagine a snake the size of this rock! Mr M always sits under that tree, must be his favourite place. I don't really have a favourite place here. At home I had the den behind the rhododendron bushes. Me and my best friend Janice used to stack our worm jars along the entrance so no one would come in. Georgie sometimes moved them though, just to annoy us. That's another thing about Akarula: there aren't any children. Maddie told me they all left before we came. Me and Georgie play with Mr M instead – not all the time, but sometimes. He knows lots of magic tricks, and stories, really good ones. Georgie thinks he's BLAST. There aren't many people Georgie thinks are BLAST. BLAST means brilliant, in case you didn't know. I'll bet he knows where she's hiding. Mr M knows things that no one else knows, secret things, things you won't find written in a book. I know a few things too. For example, his real name isn't Mr M, it is Mr Markarrwala.

The street is empty. All the women must be indoors. It's too hot to walk around. The roar of engines pulling in and out of the service station sounds like music from up here, underwater music, mixed in with the chatter of cicadas; after a while it's hard to tell which is which. I've only ever seen dead cicadas – empty dry wing shells. I think something sucks out their insides for food. Uncle Eddie says their bodies float up to heaven. Dad says they change their skins. No one really knows. I've often wondered what it must be like to know the answer to everything. Dad knows most things, but not everything. Maybe you'd just be bored because you wouldn't bother reading books, and there'd be no point talking to anyone because you'd already know whatever it was they were going to say. God must be bored, or else he makes himself forget what he knows and then goes about trying to remember things. I don't really believe in

God. But I don't not believe in him either. For all I know, God is sitting up there in the sky counting all those sucked-out cicadas.

I scan the whole place looking for Georgie, trying to get the dead cicadas out of my head. Sometimes I start to think about things, and then I can't stop. I see all these fleshy insides floating around, leaking. Hundreds of them. Thousands. I try not to breathe too much in case I suck one in by mistake. I turn around to look out the other side, the side with the service station and the last stretch of road. While I'm half-breathing, I spot my orange cardigan, way out in the bush. The cicadas disappear as I squint, trying to pick out Georgie in amongst the scrub grass. I loop a thumb and fingers around each eye, making my hands into binoculars to cut out the glare. Those cicadas still ring in my ears – they haven't gone away – I just don't see them any more. I can't see Georgie either, only my cardigan. I told her it was too hot to wear a cardigan. She doesn't listen; that's why Mum calls her Cloth Ears. I take my time climbing down. Mum told us not to cross the road because it's dangerous. Half the time I think Georgie just doesn't understand plain English.

When I get to the bottom of Red Rock Mountain I need a drink. You have to drink regularly in this heat, otherwise you'll dry out and your body will shrivel up like the cicadas. That's why we carry these water bottles. Dad's idea. We wear them over our shoulders. My strap has mice on it and my bottle is dark green. Georgie's is purple with a rabbit strap – they don't look much like rabbits if you ask me. I wanted the purple one, but Georgie made a big fuss so I said I'd have the green one instead.

The caravan door is open, and there's Dad sitting at the table reading an old *National Geographic* magazine, wearing his pyjamas and the cowboy hat Uncle Eddie gave him.

'Alright, love?' he says, putting the magazine down to scoop an ant off the table. He throws it out of the window. 'Where's Georgie?'

'Hiding.' I take a swig of water before putting my bottle under the tap. Dad nods and half-opens and closes his mouth and makes a clicking sound. 'Where's Mum?'

'In the shop.'

Dad doesn't talk much since he started taking the pink pills.

'See you later,' I tell him, screwing the top onto my bottle.

He raises his hand to the side of his head and salutes me like a sergeant major. That's Dad for you.

Once I've crossed the tarmac, I walk round behind the shop where Uncle Eddie lives. The shop is connected to Uncle Eddie's bungalow. It's got sweets and drinks, stuff for the car, that sort of thing. The bungalow behind has three rooms, not counting the bathroom: a sitting-room and two other rooms, one he uses as an office. He's not in his office; the blinds are down. I haul one of the beer crates underneath the sitting-room window and stand on it; see if I can give him a fright. He is humped on the settee in his collared t-shirt and socks. Mum is underneath him, naked, except for her neck scarf. They're doing it. One of them has knocked the water tank off Uncle Eddie's miniature model of Akarula town. They should have moved the model farther away before they started. The sight of them makes me feel sick. Mum made me promise. She said Uncle Eddie has been very good to us. She said if I go telling Dad, he'll get ill again. And then she said: you wouldn't want to be the one to make him ill, would you? I said I wouldn't, but she doesn't have to go doing it in the daytime when everyone can see. I don't bother banging on the window. All I know is that I'd never let a man do that to me.

10

I climb down off the crate and chuck it in a pile with the rest of them. Then I cross the road and pick my way through the scrub, swallowing to try and get rid of the nasty taste in my mouth. Spitting doesn't help. Each time I breathe, the heat burns the inside of my nose.

You've got to pay attention. Some of these rocks and dry grasses can slice right through you. If Georgie has gone and cut herself, I'll be in trouble. I can hear Mum already. *I told you not to take your eyes off her. What were you doing? You know she can't be left alone.* Then she'll make such a swanny about Georgie, with the plasters and the bandages, me and Dad will have to run around doing whatever Georgie wants. That's how it works. Some days I wish Georgie had never been born.

I keep walking and walking and walking. At first it's hard to remember exactly where I spotted my cardigan. It doesn't take me long though. That cardigan is like a radar. She has flung it on a rock, which means she can't be far away. If I was Georgie, I wouldn't go flinging someone else's good cardigan on a rock just because I got too hot and couldn't be bothered carrying it. Dad always says you've got to do the right thing, no matter what. I once asked him, what if you don't know which thing is the right thing? He didn't answer. He's right though. Georgie is like Mum; she doesn't care.

Two minutes later I spot Georgie's footprints in the layer of red dust that covers the sharp rocks and ground and everything else – more like smudges than footprints because of the way she twists her feet when she walks. I get this prickling feeling, sort of excited and nervous at the same time; the ground is flat; you can see as far as the horizon, and Georgie isn't visible. I start imagining things, crazy things like her being picked up by one of the huge wedge-tailed eagles and flown away. You've probably heard stories about babies getting eaten by dingoes.

Georgie's not exactly a baby though, and there aren't any dingoes that I've seen, so that's unlikely. But it is weird, the fact that I can't see her. Her footsteps carry on into the scrub.

After a while of following footsteps, I check behind me to see how far I've come. The service station looks toy-sized from here; I can hardly make out the caravan. I didn't think Georgie could walk this far. Her feet must be bleeding with all these rocks. She won't wear her special clogs, goes crazy every time Mum tries to put them on. Doesn't mind socks though. I bend down and inspect the rocks for blood or bits of clothes or fingers. What if someone has cut her up and scattered her around like bird food? You never know. I've read all sorts of stories – some of them were true. I keep on following the footprints. Nothing, nothing, nothing, and then the footprints stop.

There is a hole, partly covered over with old nailed-together wooden planks. The wood must have been rotten because some of it has fallen in on top of Georgie. I can only just make her out at the bottom of the hole. It's a long way down. Her body is all scrunched up, and one of her legs is cocked out at a funny angle; she's got her arm twisted up in her water bottle strap. There is not much room down there: the size of an airing cupboard, maybe smaller. I picture those posters, the ones that say *WANTED – DEAD OR ALIVE*, with Georgie's head on. As I skirt around the edge for something to pull her out with, I notice more wooden plank covers, all with x marks on the top in flaking yellow paint. This must be why Mum told us not to cross the road. When I asked her what was dangerous about it, she said *it just is*, which is what she always says when she doesn't know the answer. I call down to Georgie to wait on. 'Don't move,' I tell her, and she waves up at me, flapping her arms and one of her legs, opening and closing her mouth, doing her fish impression. I can't tell, with the glare of sun and all the shadow, whether she is smiling or not.

12

This thin shiver slides right down my back. I have to hold my breath to get rid of it. When I let go and breathe again, I tell Georgie, 'Mum's going to kill you when she finds out you crossed the road on your own.' Georgie lets out a grunt that turns into a moan and then drops to a kind of whisper, ending up in a stutter like this: aaadropddwwwwwwwwrrlllL.

I find a smooth rock to sit on while I work out what to do next. Georgie carries on making queer sounds. I wave at her, throwing my cap and cardigan down the hole so that she can use them. That was a mistake.

There are things you ought to know. When Georgie was born, Mum nearly died because the doctor couldn't get Georgie out. I don't know if her head was too big or what it was. Mum was fifteen days in hospital. Dad and me had to clean Georgie's smelly bum and try to stop her screaming until Mum came home. That was more or less the start of it. We stopped going to Granny and Grandpa's house in Whitley Bay. Dad said there was no time and Mum said there was no money. No one could work out why Georgie stared into space, wouldn't feed properly, and spasmed all the time. If something wound her up, she just stopped breathing.

Take bathtimes. Any normal baby enjoys a bath, blows bubbles, scoots the plastic duck around. I know; I've seen them. Not Georgie. She dives underneath the water and flaps her arms and legs about, making out she's some kind of fish. I have to watch her all the time to make sure she doesn't drown. One time I left her too long and we had to call an ambulance. Was I in trouble for that! I used to get in trouble even when it wasn't my fault, except when Uncle Eddie was around. When he was visiting, you could do almost anything, and all you'd get from Mum was a raised eyebrow and maybe a quick don't-do-that-again smack.

Uncle Eddie came to visit us in England last summer. It was July or August, the summer holidays anyway. I was in the front garden pushing Georgie around the lawn in a go-cart Dad had made out of fruit crates.

'Arreeeeeeeeba arreeeeeeeeeeeeba arrrrrrrrreeeeeeeeeeeeeeee-baaaaaaaaaaaaa!' Georgie was shouting and hitting me with a stick to make me go faster. When it got to be my turn, she said she didn't want to play. She wasn't strong enough to push me around anyway. Dad was in bed – he spent a lot of time in bed after he stopped working full-time for the newspaper – and Mum was doing something in the kitchen. Our neighbourhood wasn't rough, but we didn't get limousines driving down West Street every day, so when this white one pulled up outside the gate, I was pretty flabbergasted. (Flabbergasted is one of my favourite words.) First of all I thought it was Madonna. I'd seen her on the television getting out of the exact same car. Georgie was squealing and snorting, nearly wetting herself to get out of the go-cart and scab a look. The back door of the limousine opened and a man stepped onto the pavement in these spit-clean shoes. I didn't recognise him at first. He asked me where he might find Monica Harvey, and winked at me. That's when I knew it was Uncle Eddie. Then he shook my hand and asked if I remembered him. I did, except that he looked different all dressed up. You should have heard him: this strange twangy accent that made him sound like he'd swallowed a loose guitar string. He introduced himself to Georgie, but she just stared at him. She probably couldn't get over the fact that he'd shaken my hand and not so much as whistled at her first. I led him into the hall because Georgie didn't have the manners.

Mum came out of the kitchen once she heard our voices. She must have been flabbergasted too because she dropped her tea-towel, turned bright red, and stuttered a bit before she got her words out.

'Eddie! What are you doing here? Why didn't you let us know you were coming?' All said in that high-pitched *oh my goodness* tone she puts on when she's surprised.

'Caroline!' Uncle Eddie said, gripping Mum around her waist and spinning her. One of her sandals flew off and hit my head. Georgie giggled, until I kicked her in the shin. 'What do you think?' He plucked at his trousers and did a half-turn.

Mum picked the grass out of my hair while she said, 'You haven't changed a bit.'

'You're even more beautiful.' Uncle Eddie smiled; you could tell he had brushed his teeth.

I showed Mum the limousine. 'It's got six doors,' I said, trying to get a proper look at it – Uncle Eddie was in the way.

'Some style you have,' Mum said, eyeing Uncle Eddie up and down and peering over his shoulder on her tiptoes. 'This isn't Hollywood, you know.' In his suit and tie and thin-striped shirt, he looked like a newsreader.

'Had a meeting in London. Thought I'd drive up and collect you. Fly you back to Oz. Can't seem to convince you on paper.'

Mum put her sandal back on and said, 'It's not me you need to convince. You know what Michael's like. Complains if I get a different brand of milk.'

'How is he?'

'Same as ever. God, it's good to see you.'

The two of them carried on like this, ignoring me and Georgie. Mum took Uncle Eddie's jacket and laid it on the dresser while he explained about these houses he was building. He went on and on about a place called Akarula. Then they walked off into the lounge arm in arm. I took the car keys from Uncle Eddie's jacket pocket and went back outside.

'Give them,' Georgie whined.

I opened the car and slipped into the driver's seat. It took Georgie all of two seconds to get in beside me.

That was some car. The back seat was practically a sofa, and there was a telly and curtains and a mini bar. I turned the wheel and we were off. We drove to America, India, Madagascar, and plenty of other places. I told Georgie about the animals we could see, pointing out the odd tree and high-rise building. We waved at passing cars, winding the window down because the weather was so hot. She added her own stuff, but mostly stuck to things in the town. Georgie even got car sick – that's how real she thought our trip was – all over Uncle Eddie's map. We had to get out in the end because the car stank. I slammed the door shut. It wasn't my fault Georgie left her thumb in the way. She didn't throw a wobbly; the shock of it took her voice away.

After I'd put the keys back in Uncle Eddie's jacket pocket, I washed Georgie's face upstairs and strapped a plaster round her thumb. That's when I promised that if anyone asked, I'd say it was me who got sick on the map. I think her thumb must have really hurt because her face turned see-through blue. Mum had to drive her down to Doctor Sutton's later on. The thing with Georgie is, when she gets upset or ill, she stops breathing. That's why she nearly died a hundred million times. So if she asks you to do something, you have to do it. She asked me to steal a fiver from Uncle Eddie's wallet, so I did.

Dad had woken up by then. All three of them were drinking wine in the lounge and laughing a lot. Well, Mum and Uncle Eddie were laughing. We all laughed in the three days Uncle Eddie stayed with us, even Georgie, who didn't like visitors; she usually swelled up like a puffer fish until they went home. The thing I liked about Uncle Eddie was that he didn't make a song and dance about Georgie. He didn't know that any minute she could die and, if he wasn't careful, it would be his fault. Nobody told him. Uncle Eddie kept picking me up and flying me around over his head, saying *this is what the plane ride to Australia is like.* He didn't tell anyone about Georgie getting sick, or his missing money. I didn't get in trouble about Georgie's thumb either. Mum said, *accidents happen,* just like that, and didn't even ask what we were doing in Uncle Eddie's car. Usually Mum would want the whole story before deciding what to do with me. Instead she played her guitar and made up songs, something she hadn't done in ages. They were good songs too. Me and Georgie danced around the lounge. I had my spinning skirt on. Dad watched us, and clicked his false tooth up and down to make us laugh. Uncle Eddie taped the whole thing on his brand new cine-camera.

That week Dad was doing film reviews at the cinema, which meant we got free tickets. Dad could tell you who was in any film that was ever made, when it was made, how long it was, the whole lot. On the Friday night Uncle Eddie stayed with us, we walked into town to see *E.T.* I showed Uncle Eddie Wogan's Bookshop as we went past; it was closed, so we didn't go in. Uncle Eddie pretended he was a B52 bomber plane and flew down the street with his arms stretched out, shooting at me and Mum until we fell over, making this pa pa pa pa pa sound for the bullets. It was fun, although Dad's games were better. Dad's games were real games. With Uncle Eddie, everything was made up. Dad didn't play much of anything now though; he was either too tired or too busy on his typewriter. Georgie didn't want to play the plane game. When she saw Mum and me lying on the pavement, she started making this whirring noise like a fire engine. It took Mum ages to calm her down. Georgie must have thought we were dead. We walked normally after that.

The cinema was packed because it was the first night of *E.T.* Dad had saved us the best seats, six rows back, right in the middle. He always got there early so that he could sit in his favourite seat – F14. In the interval, a woman in a paper hat and tinted glasses brought around ice-creams and drinks, the same woman who had ripped our tickets at the door.

Georgie wouldn't sit properly on her seat. She kept slipping onto the floor and rubbing her legs against the carpet until they were red sore. Which is why we didn't have carpets at home. Mum had to keep pulling her up, but once the film got started, she just left her there. I loved that film. In the bit where they take E.T. to the science hospital, I stood up and shouted when E.T.'s heart glowed again. I was so glad he was alive. I don't know what I shouted; I just wanted him to get away. Mum leaned over and pulled me back into my chair, handing me a liquorice allsort.

'It's just a story,' she whispered. It's not real.' But it *was* real; it was happening right there in front of me. Uncle Eddie must have thought it was real too because at the end of the film he was crying. When I passed him my handkerchief, he said, 'That was some film,' and blew his nose twice.

Dad had to stay behind to meet one of the newspaper men, so we said goodnight to him on the steps outside. On the way home, Uncle Eddie said he was going to build a cinema for Dad in Akarula. He was always saying things like that.

I asked him where Akarula was on the world map. (I know the world map off by heart.)

'A long way from here,' he said. 'Why don't you come and visit?'

I said I would. Then Uncle Eddie made me promise. I had to spit on my hand and shake his hand three times, like the Red Indians do in *Sworn Away*. Mum was busy inspecting the carpet patterns on Georgie's legs underneath the street lamp outside Woolworths, so she didn't see me promise.

The day before Uncle Eddie left, he took us out for lunch. We all got dressed up. Dad was wearing his wedding suit and Mum was in her best mauve dress. Me and Georgie wore the matching velvet skirts we got for Christmas, even though it was summer. As we were leaving, Uncle Eddie asked Dad to drive.

'We'll take the scenic route. There's 400ccs of horse power in that little lady.'

Dad was holding onto the coat stand. I knew he didn't really want to go.

Mum said, 'I can drive,' the way she always said *I can drive*, and snapped up the car keys from the bowl on the dresser before she went outside.

'I might stay here,' Dad said, resting one of his hands on my shoulder and giving it a squeeze.

Uncle Eddie slapped Dad's arm. 'Come on, Mike. My treat.'

Mum came back in for Georgie's shoes. She could see what was happening. 'Don't spoil it for everyone,' she said to Dad, not quite looking at him. That meant he was in trouble.

Dad heaved a sigh out of his chest and slowly shrank, like a punctured balloon. His hand went limp on my shoulder. I took hold of it and kissed it and held on to his fingers.

'We're going out for lunch. It's booked. Let's go. Come on, skunk.' Uncle Eddie called me skunk sometimes. I didn't really like it. He strode outside, and Mum and Georgie followed. I thought they were going to go without us, but Uncle Eddie marched back in and stood so close to Dad their noses nearly touched. 'This isn't fair, Mike,' he said through his teeth. 'Just get in the car.'

Dad told me to go outside, and edged me towards the door, which Uncle Eddie closed behind me. I could still hear them talking though, as if they were trying to knock each other over with their voices. It was Dad's voice that kept falling down. Eventually they both came out.

Uncle Eddie said 'Let's cruise,' as he caught the car keys Mum threw at him and slid into the driver's seat. On the way to the restaurant, he told us about opal stones and how if you look at them for long enough, they turn into the sea. What he meant was, they *look* like the sea. The sea at Whitley Bay is grey, and in the winter it looks black. Most stones are grey or black anyway. I couldn't see why Uncle Eddie thought opals were so special. Dad only spoke once, just as we went past the cinema. He said, 'They've made this into a one-way street.'

That restaurant wasn't like the Berni Inn where we went for our birthdays. There were silver knives and forks, padded chairs, and a tablecloth which matched the napkins. Mum noticed that the napkins were the same colour as the carpet and the curtains. It was hard to decide what to eat. I ordered the third thing on the menu, which was basically fish and chips, only they'd written *fillet of plaice with French fries*. Georgie had the same. We all got green soup to start.

The waiter was a tall skinny Frenchman who wore white gloves and a white apron and smiled a lot. He had the exact same smile as Uncle Eddie.

'What will we drink to?' Uncle Eddie said, raising his glass of champagne.

'Australia?' Mum said, looking at Dad with an upside-down grin. And then she chinked glasses with Uncle Eddie. Georgie held up her glass of orange juice and chinked too. Dad didn't feel like chinking. Me neither.

'How's the writing?' Uncle Eddie asked, passing Dad some bread. 'I think you're in the wrong game. What you bringing in? Twenty, thirty grand?'

'Try halving it,' Mum said into her napkin.

Uncle Eddie carried on talking to Dad. 'I'm not trying to tell my older brother what to do. But the property market in Oz is about to soar. All you need is a bit of savvy and a few contacts. I could set you up. Plus the fact that you'd love it out there.' He took up his bread roll and ripped it in half as he turned to Mum. 'Why don't we all drive down to Whitley? Your folks wouldn't mind a quick visit?'

'They'd be delighted,' Mum said. Her cheeks were pink from the champagne.

'It's too long a drive for Georgie,' Dad said, laying his spoon down next to his bowl and wiping his mouth on the fancy napkin. 'Can you pass me another roll, please?'

Mum looked from Uncle Eddie to Dad and said, 'We don't all have to go.'

'If you like,' Dad said flatly. He filled up Uncle Eddie's glass. The bubbles nearly spilt over.

'Come to London with me?' Uncle Eddie said to Dad, nearly jumping out of his chair with excitement. 'You can check out the national papers, show them your articles, boost yourself up a bit.' Uncle Eddie reminded me of next-door's dog, the one that always tried to sniff your knickers.

'Leave it, Eddie,' Dad said, putting on a weak smile. 'We don't all want what you have.'

Mum said something underneath her breath and then gulped down the rest of her drink. She had a lipstick smudge on her front tooth but I didn't bother telling her.

'Course not. I'd just love you to see it. Think about it. That's all I'm asking. How's Terry doing? Must call in while I'm here.'

Terry was our next-door neighbour who owned the knicker-sniffing dog. He was pretty old and smelly, but he always gave us Fry's chocolate mint bars, and there was a giant snow globe on his windowsill that he'd let you shake if you agreed to comb his hair. Georgie liked the globe. She never combed Terry's hair though; it was always me who had to do that.

'Is it like Disneyland?' Georgie asked. We were all amazed because Georgie didn't speak normally, not in public. She'd talk to me if we were on our own, or to Mum and Dad, if she wanted something, but I'd never heard her say anything when we were out. Most people thought she was deaf and dumb. Uncle Eddie didn't even blink.

'Akarula? You could say that.' And then he went on about the town and the people and what they did and how many houses he had and how much we'd like the weather. He made everything sound so important. I imagined Australia to be black and white, like a newspaper: not many pictures, and that small neat print. Dad's stories were always interesting.

Georgie stopped listening to Uncle Eddie. Because she was twisting the buttons on her cardigan, Mum got cross and slapped her hand away; then she gave Georgie her gold wedding ring to play with so that Georgie wouldn't cry.

I asked Uncle Eddie what kinds of animals there were in Akarula. He gave me a whole list. Dad knew even more. I'd heard of kangaroos and wallabies. In my notebook I did a few sketches and wrote down most of the names while I was waiting for my main course.

The food was served on plates the size of car wheels, and there wasn't much of it. Georgie finished hers, which was the first time she'd ever finished a plate of food. She was in a great mood. We played 'I Spy' at the table; I won and she didn't even try to win back. Only at the end, when the rest of us were eating our chocolate mousse, she slid off her chair and started doing her floor dance, rubbing her legs against the carpet, getting fluff all over her velvet skirt. That's when Mum stood up and said it was time to go home. I had to look after Georgie until the waiter brought the bill. It came on a saucer with some chocolates, which Mum stuffed in her handbag. Dad took the bill and pulled his wallet out of his back pocket.

Uncle Eddie said, 'This is my shout, Mike,' but Dad insisted. He said, 'You don't have to pay for everything.'

Mum got all cockadoodled. 'You can't afford this,' she said to Dad. 'That's more than a week's wages.' The waiter took Dad's card and brought it back on the same saucer, only there were no chocolates this time. Uncle Eddie left a £10 note under the sugar bowl. He tried to slip Dad some money on the way out, but Dad got cross, so Uncle Eddie held the door open for him instead.

Georgie let Uncle Eddie squeeze her hand on the way home while we were stopped at the traffic lights. He called her his Strawberry Girl, probably because her favourite fruit is strawberries, or at least one of her favourite fruits; she likes peaches too, but only if the skins are peeled off.

'You're privileged,' Mum said.

'She's right to be choosy.' Uncle Eddie winked at Mum in the rear-view mirror.

Georgie told me later that Uncle Eddie was BLAST. I said I thought he was OK. When Uncle Eddie was around, everyone behaved differently; it was a bit like being on holiday. He came down to Wogan's with me later that day. We found a book on Australian wildlife, a big hardback, and Uncle Eddie bought it for me. While Mrs Wogan was wrapping up the book, Uncle Eddie told her she had the smile of a movie star. She drew a sort of squiggle with her body and smiled even more. The next day, when I went in to spend Uncle Eddie's fiver, she said: 'Your Uncle's very handsome.' I told her that he wasn't half as handsome as the lead singer of Showaddywaddy.

Oh, and Mum went back to the restaurant to find her wedding ring, the one Georgie had been messing around with. She didn't find it though.

On the last night, Uncle Eddie went with Mum to the country club to watch her sing and came back drunk, shouting out her songs at the top of his voice, waking us all up. In the morning he told Mum she was going to be a big hit, said he'd sort her out with a record deal as soon as he got back to Australia. Mum told him to stop talking nonsense, but she wasn't cross. She reminded him of what Grandpa had told her (that was Mum's dad): *singers are either drug addicts or drunks.* They both laughed. When Uncle Eddie asked her to sing his favourite song, she did, right there in the kitchen, in her quilted dressing gown.

The next day Uncle Eddie drove Mum to Whitley Bay in the limousine. Mum thought it was best if I stayed and helped Dad with Georgie, so I wrote a letter to Granny and Grandpa instead. I could have gone, if it hadn't been for Georgie.

After Uncle Eddie flew back to Australia, Mum went on so much about Akarula and the sun and all the rest of it that Dad said we were going nowhere and if he heard another word he'd … he'd … he'd do something – he hadn't worked out exactly what. That put an end to the talking. For at least a week Mum didn't speak to Dad. And then the letter came. We were at the breakfast table. Georgie had a rash on her face and Mum was dabbing cream on with a cotton bud. Dad was reading the newspaper. He got up to answer the door: a special delivery that had to be signed for, a large brown envelope addressed to The Harvey Family. Dad stood by the sink with his mouth hanging open as he read through the papers inside. Somewhere between throwing them at Mum and sinking down into his chair, he let out a kind of wet dog-cry, and then with what was left of his voice said: 'What the hell is this?' holding up a cheque he'd obviously found in the envelope, waving it in front of Mum's face like a pair of dirty knickers. Mum put down the cotton bud and took a few deep shaky breaths before she spoke.

'I gave Eddie a call. If we don't like it, we'll just come back.'

'Just come back?'

Mum snatched the cheque from Dad's hand and told him not to get worked up. His face and neck had patches of purple on and he was juddering as he said: 'We'll get the house, if that's what you want. I'll borrow some money until we get sorted.' He pushed his hands against the table to steady himself. I thought he might need some pills so I got a box from the dresser in the hall and put them down in front of him while Mum carried on.

'I don't want to live in a house we can't afford.' (She'd seen this house for sale in Johnstown, a yellow one with huge windows and a balcony, about twice the size of our house.) She was getting all huffy and her hands had bunched up into fists. 'We're the ones who have to live with it; it's not just you. If we stay here, nothing will change.'

She yanked the cotton bud out of Georgie's mouth as Dad took his hands off the table and let them fall into his lap. He hadn't touched his pills. I wanted to say that it was alright, that it wasn't his fault. I felt sorry for Dad. He got blamed for everything, unless it was my fault, and even then he always stepped in and rescued me. Dad was staring at the butter dish. By the time I'd worked out exactly what I wanted to say, he was talking again.

'I might be doing a story for *The Times*.'

'When was the last time we had a holiday?' Mum asked.

I knew the answer to that. 'Before Georgie was born,' I said. I was going to add that Mum had been to Whitley Bay with Uncle Eddie for the night, but I didn't get a chance.

'Exactly.' Mum was still looking at Dad as if he had answered her. 'Think about the girls. It's a great opportunity for them.'

'Can we leave it, please?'

Mum got up and started clearing plates off the table and stacking them beside the sink. Over the clattering she said, 'This isn't just your decision.'

'What's wrong with this house?'

Mum looked like she was on the verge of tears when she turned around. Her hands were clutching at the edge of the sink behind her. 'I'm so tired,' she said. I thought she was going to go on, but she just stood there with her mouth open.

I decided not to say anything, but I was thinking I would like to see a koala bear and a kangaroo. I'd been reading about Australian animals in that book Uncle Eddie had bought me: tree frogs with gold marks on their foreheads, poisonous redback spiders, flying fruit bats, giant worms. And then there was the fact that I'd promised Uncle Eddie. We'd spat and shaken on it.

'What about school?' Dad asked.

'Moni's already a year ahead.'

'Maybe next year. We could save up.'

'Can't you see what's happening?' Mum was really upset now. She had turned back round to the sink and kept banging the plates into the drying rack so that they slammed against each other. Georgie didn't like the way Mum was going on, so she bum-shuffled over to the fish tank and pressed her face right up against the glass. Usually that calmed her down. Dad stood up, balancing himself against the table. For a while he didn't say anything, and then he whispered, 'We can't accept this kind of money.'

I knew it wouldn't be long before he gave in.

I think about all this as I'm sitting by the mineshaft. A small light flickers at the corner of my eye and won't go away. My head is pounding. Georgie isn't grateful for my cap or my cardigan. She's making a racket down there, giving me a right headache. As I stand up, my legs collapse. It takes three attempts before I can stay upright. Sitting for so long in this heat without my hat has made me dizzy. The ripples of sun dancing in front of me make everything look skew-whiff. Before I leave, I tell Georgie I am going to fetch a rope. I don't say goodbye; I just head off, picking my way back through the bush, trying not to fall. It's not easy. The rocks keep jumping up, tripping me over, and the tight air clings to my skin. I can hardly breathe. Hot and cold and white shivery. My head burns and swims and feels as if at any minute it might turn into a jumbo jet and just fly off.

Finally I reach the tarmac of the service station. I start looking for a piece of rope. I get so mad and knotted up inside, I can't see straight. Then I throw up on the heap of tyres at the edge of the scrub. Flies swarm in on my sick and I throw up again. After that my legs melt away and all the lights go out.

It is already dark when I hear Dad's voice and realise I'm in the caravan. He lifts up my head, giving me sips of water, and asks me where Georgie is. I'm covered with cold wet towels. 'Is she with Mum?' He tells me not to worry, says I'll be alright. He doesn't know. Every time I try to speak, the words slip off my tongue. Dad presses a damp sponge against my face. The water runs into my eyes, wets my hair and dribbles down my chin. 'Keep drinking,' he says.

His voice gets farther away and the strip light flashes on and off. I can't seem to keep my eyes open. Maybe I'm sleeping, although my head is still awake. Orange rain. My glass body full of tiny blue birds. Rainbow fish with fingers and toes. And Georgie shrinking and shrinking until she disappears. Like magic.

More voices. 'I thought she was with you.'

'Why didn't you check?'

Someone shakes me. There is a sharp pain in my shoulders. When I open my eyes, Mum's face is red and twisted. She pulls me up. Then she throws me back down onto the cushions and shouts: 'Where's Georgie?' My mouth has crusted over. 'Moni!' she screams. When I manage to sit up, I force myself to talk and all the bits and pieces of the day spill out in the wrong order until finally I get to say, 'We were playing hide and seek.' Mum traps the air in her mouth with both hands. Dad puts on his boots and rummages through the drawer for a torch. I carry on. 'She's got my cap.' I tell the bit about the mineshaft and how I was trying to find a rope. I don't get to the part where I was sick because Mum tilts her head back and lets out a wailing sound which leaves the air shuddering. When the air finally stills, she says to Dad, 'Let's go. Georgie hates being in the dark.' She says the last bit to herself. It's true, Georgie does hate the dark; she has to sleep with the glow-light on. Mum doesn't need to yank my arm like that though. Dad never hurts me, even when he's cross.

'Don't be ridiculous,' Dad says, stepping in between me and Mum. 'She can't go out like that.' As he looks at me, draped in the towels, his face cracks.

Mum persists. 'How do you expect to find her? There are hundreds of shafts. We can't afford to waste time. She's been out there for hours.'

I sling on my water bottle. Dad doesn't stop me. His hands are shaking as he helps me off the cushions.

'Can you stand?' he asks softly. 'Take it steady. I can always carry you.' He turns to Mum and says, 'You'd better call the doctor. I'll take Eddie with me. One of us should stay here, just in case.'

As Dad closes the caravan door behind us, the kettle starts whistling.

Outside, the night air prickles my skin. Dad holds my hand as we walk towards the pumps. With a few deep breaths, the fog in my head clears. I can see a whole range of stars. At the carwash buckets, Dad says, 'Wait here. I won't be long.' He presses his hand against my forehead before he runs over to Uncle Eddie's house for a rope. I feel strange; it's like my arms and legs aren't in the right place and my head has slipped off to one side. For a while I think I'm going to be sick again. I bend over and keep breathing until eventually the sickness sinks back down. Then I straighten up and count stars for a while, which makes me feel better.

There are hundreds of stars. This sky is bigger than the sky in England. In my space book it says that stars are suns; each one is different. They are not all white, even though they look white. Vega in Lyra, for example, is steely blue. And the Australian sky has different star constellations from the English sky. Australia hasn't got the Plough or the Hunting Dogs. They've got the Kite and the Jewel Box instead. I find the Kite, but I can't find the Jewel Box.

Dad returns with a rope slung over his shoulder. Uncle Eddie is right behind him, adjusting the beam on his torch. 'Alright, Monica?' He points his torch right in my face, blinding me. I ask him if he can show me the Jewel Box. He switches off the torch and looks up at the sky, but Dad says 'Let's go' and marches on, flashing his own torch ahead of us. Uncle Eddie and I have to run to keep up with him as he speeds across the road and starts tramping through the bush.

'What were you doing? You know this area is out of bounds.' Uncle Eddie catches his leg against some scrub grass as he speaks to me, interrupting himself to curse out loud.

'Hide and seek. I told Georgie not to leave the service station.'

'I'd say she's won the game at this point.'

Dad stops for a second, bending down to study my face. He tells Uncle Eddie to give me a piggy-back while he goes on ahead. It's not so easy to find the mineshaft, but I keep pointing forwards. Somehow I remember. Somehow I just know which way to go. And then I don't.

'We're going round in circles. Are you sure this is right?' Uncle Eddie twists his head round to look at me. His face loses its shape in the dark and his teeth shine like fish eyes.

I tell him I want to get down. It feels as if there is something punching behind my forehead. Uncle Eddie sets me on the ground and Dad clutches my face in his hands and says 'Don't worry, love. You're doing fine. We just need to find that shaft. Can you remember what you were looking at when you came back? Were the petrol pumps on this side or that side?'

I tell him how it was: the cars looking matchbox size, the distant outline of the pumps, the way I could hardly see the caravan. Even in the dark, the service station stands out, like the edge of a shadow, darker than the starlit sky. That helps. We head across the scrub, to the right, and I find the spot where the picture of the service station fits into place. Uncle Eddie walks back, just in case we've already missed the hole, and me and Dad go on together, holding hands. We nearly fall into the mineshaft.

'That's it!' I yell, pointing at the dark hole in the ground.

Dad calls back to Uncle Eddie before he drops onto his hands and knees. He slings the rope on the ground beside him and pulls away what is left of the rotten wood, shining his torch inside the hole.

I found it! My heart races, beating in my mouth, in my ears, underneath my t-shirt. I want to let out a huge cry that would curve in the sky like a giant rainbow. But then my heart stops. The hole is empty.

'Maybe she climbed out,' I suggest, half-expecting to see Georgie standing beside me when I look round. Uncle Eddie is coming towards us.

Dad says, 'Are you sure this is the one? They're all the same.' But as he spins the beam of the torch around the bottom of the hole again, I catch sight of a piece of orange cardigan. I point down to the sleeve of wool that somehow disappears into the side of the hole.

Uncle Eddie is breathing fast as he crouches beside me. His body touches mine. The skin on his arm is warm and hairy; it tickles. I move closer to Dad.

'She must have gone down a tunnel,' Uncle Eddie announces, when he finally catches his breath. 'It's a rabbit warren round here.'

'You didn't say anything about tunnels,' Dad's voice breaks up, crackling like the ones on the radio.

'It's a mine. What do you expect?' Uncle Eddie wipes his nose on the back of his hand as he takes another look down the shaft, swirling the torch beam around the hole with his other hand. 'She can't be far away.'

'Geoooooooorgie!' I shout. Uncle Eddie stops talking and looks at me. I call again and again; Dad and Uncle Eddie join in. Then we listen, holding our breath; we wait for a reply. We walk from shaft to shaft. Uncle Eddie hauls the lids off, Dad shines his torch down, we all shout. The shafts are everywhere and each one looks the same as the one before.

The sky is pale pink when Dad carries me back to the caravan. Through half-closed eyes, I can see three galahs balanced on the telegraph wires, waiting for their morning feed. My body is so heavy with tiredness, it has sunk right into Dad's chest; I can't tell whether the heartbeat thumping between us is his or mine.

Dad lays me down on the cushions in the caravan and covers me with the crochet blanket. He watches as I drink a glass of water, then he sinks down on the edge of the double bed next to Mum at the other end of the caravan. Mum is sitting straight-backed, staring out of the window; Georgie's red clogs are nestled in her lap. The cigarette lodged between her fingers has burnt to ash. Dad removes it carefully, throwing it into the sink. He hates smoking. He once said to Mum that she gave herself away by smoking, whatever that meant. All of a sudden she springs to life.

'Where is she? Has the doctor arrived?'

'It'll be easier to find her with some light.'

Mum opens and closes her mouth just like Georgie does, and then she stops blinking.

'She's in one of the tunnels,' Dad says.

Mum is about to say something but then stops mid-breath. She starts trembling and gasps for air as if she is trying to breathe under water. 'It was over ninety degrees yesterday.' She watches Dad change the batteries in the torch. 'What if…?' She doesn't manage to finish.

'She's smarter than we think. You've always said that.' Dad attempts to give me a smile before he leaves.

'I'll come with you,' I say, sitting up too quickly, catching my shoulder on the flip-down table.

Mum looks up from fastening her sandals and stares at me for a second. I swing my legs down underneath the table and press my feet against the floor. My shoulder aches and tingles, but the rest of me feels numb. I can't tell whether my feet have stopped at the floor or are still sinking down. Although Mum is only a few steps away, she might as well be on the other side of the world.

'Get some sleep,' she growls. 'You've done enough already.' She slams the door shut and runs to catch up with Dad.

I listen to the drone of the fan and let my eyes rest on the crisscross pattern of the curtains. Everyone else must be sleeping. They have no idea all this is going on. In my mind I am packing up so that when Mum and Dad get back with Georgie, we can go straight home. I carry on staring at the crisscross pattern until the lines start touching each other. My water bottle feels heavy; the strap presses into my shoulder, but I can't seem to move.

It's hard to say how long it is before the engines start up, drivers' voices and radio songs spilling out of the open truck windows. The air floods with petrol fumes. I try to picture our house in England: the postcards of animals on my bedroom wall, the wooden banisters, my books, Georgie's green rocking chair. I try to wish everything back to normal. All I can see is part of the curtain that hides the bulk of Red Rock Mountain.

I get out my notebook and write a page and a half for yesterday and half a page for today, making a pencil sketch of my orange cardigan in the margin of the last page: just the cardigan, hanging there on its own. And then I see clearly all the mineshafts filling up with water and Georgie flapping like a fish. She is calling me. For a moment I feel as if I'm floating. Her open mouth sucks me in and I am diving down a long dark hole. I didn't mean to, I tell her. It wasn't my fault. I keep falling, can't stop; I try to catch the water as I go but the drops slip through my fingers, and I see faces, hundreds of lost faces behind a glass door, begging me to let them out. I have the key. I can feel it in my pocket. If I open the door, we'll all drown. Don't open it. The key has a life of its own. One two three four five pink pills, not pink but grey and pink, flying down my throat. Will someone feed those birds?

Uncle Eddie lifts me off the caravan floor and talks to me as he carries me across the sunny tarmac, past the petrol pumps, through the service station shop and into his sitting room. In my head I see Mr M doing his magic trick where he stands so still he turns into a tree, and no matter where you look, you can't find him. The tree and Mr M are the same: tall, crooked, and lonely. I have never noticed that before.

When I open my eyes, Uncle Eddie is taking off my boots and socks. 'What were you doing on the floor? I've got enough to worry about without you playing dead. That's a charmer of a bruise on your cheek.' He lays me on the settee and tucks a jumper underneath my head for a pillow.

Georgie! I point to the model of Akarula on the coffee table. Uncle Eddie can't see her. She is walking in between the buildings, so small she fits through the tiny doors of the cinema Uncle Eddie will build for Dad in a year or two.

The doctor examines me. Her hair is cut close and she is dressed in the dry browns of the bush. Not pretty, though her eyes sparkle behind her gold-rimmed glasses and she smiles all the time.

She tells Uncle Eddie that I'm out of the worst. 'A bad dose of sunstroke. Keep her hydrated. Plenty of rest, plenty of fluids. If her temperature goes up again, give her a cold bath, and if you're still worried, have her flown out to the hospital.' When she's put everything back in her bag, she pulls a boiled sweet from her trouser pocket and presses it into my hand. 'A bit of sugar to perk you up.' She winks at me. I like this doctor better than our English doctor. Doctor Sutton's breath used to smell of cheese mould and his hands were always cold.

I tell the doctor about Georgie being stuck in the cinema until Uncle Eddie butts in. 'I don't think Susan's got time to hear about that now.'

The doctor is about to speak when Uncle Eddie steers her out of the room, stepping into the hall after her.

As he closes the door, she says 'I didn't know you had a niece.'

Uncle Eddie's voice isn't so clear. He says something about being *full of surprises* and *if only*. I get up and accidentally lean on the door handle and it clicks open a little. Although they are whispering, I hear every word. Uncle Eddie tells the doctor about Georgie. She says she already knows. She says, 'What did they say about the others?'

'I haven't told them yet.'

'You haven't told them? What are you waiting for?'

'It's bad enough already.'

The doctor coughs before she says, 'We both know it's going to get a lot worse. They have to understand what they're up against. You have to tell them before someone else does.'

'What are they up against?'

'Eddie...'

They go into the shop and once that door closes their voices cut out. I try to understand what's been said, only whichever way I play it back, it makes no sense. The doctor must be Uncle Eddie's friend. That's all I know.

I roll onto my side and concentrate on the model town. When Uncle Eddie gets back, I tell him right away: 'There are too many houses on your model.'

'In Australia, people move houses around. We'll get them back again one day,' he says, and then he tests me. 'What does that stand for?' He points to the sign on the model by the pylon.

'Electricity.'

'Blue?'

'Water supply.'

'Green?'

Each building is colour-coded. Uncle Eddie must think I've got a short memory because he tests me all the time.

'Do you want to help me with something?' he asks.

35

He goes into his office, coming back with a wad of envelopes, and sits down next to me. Then he starts writing cheques. I have to put them in the envelopes for him and seal them. When he has written the last cheque, he kisses the back of it and passes it to me. I wipe his kiss off on my t-shirt before I put the cheque inside the envelope and lick the seal.

Uncle Eddie's eyes are alight, like a motorway, with hundreds of speeding thoughts racing through them. He gets up and goes over to the mini fridge where he keeps the beer, flipping the top off one of the stubby bottles. After taking a long gulp, he slams the bottle down on the counter and his eyes grow even bigger, as if he's been hit by a giant brain wave.

'I'll deliver these today, before anyone starts getting ideas.' Uncle Eddie carries on mumbling to himself, thinking aloud. I can't make out half of what he's saying. Eventually I interrupt.

'She can't get out.' I point at the cinema.

'Who can't get out?'

'Georgie. They've locked the doors.'

Uncle Eddie screws up his eyes and smiles a small smile. 'Your mum and dad should be back soon.'

'She's in the cinema. I saw her.'

He stares at me for a moment, and then kneels down beside the model. 'What is she watching?'

'*The Wizard of Oz.*'

He rests back on his heels and lets his eyes skip about the room. 'At least someone's having fun.' Fixing his eyes on the model, he starts mumbling again, something about the town, I can't make it out; I don't even want to. When Uncle Eddie goes on like this, his voice settles into a thin grey line. I imagine walking that line, like a tightrope, just for fun.

I tug at his arm to get his attention back before I say: 'She's afraid of the witch.'

'We're all afraid of that witch. Why don't you ask Georgie where she's hiding?'

'She's in there.' I point at the cinema again.

'Alright then, we'd best get her out.' He reaches down and pretends to open the cinema doors, which are about the size of his thumb.

'They're locked,' I tell him. He doesn't believe me. I hardly believe myself, but I saw her; she went straight through the doors.

'Well then, let's find the key.' He rummages around in his pocket and pulls out the key to the shop and hands it to me.

'That's the shop key.' I can't breathe fast enough. Georgie is trying to breathe too. 'You'll be alright. Don't worry,' I tell her. The inside of my body changes colour from green to black to freezing blue. Uncle Eddie jumps up and goes over to the window.

'I'll sort it out,' he says, spinning round and shooting out through the door. I can hear him in the shop, talking to the woman who works on Saturdays. She is asking about Georgie.

'The women went out early. At least they know what to do,' the woman says.

Uncle Eddie doesn't tell her that Georgie is in the cinema. When he comes back again, he's got another key.

'This should do it,' he says, hunching down beside the model, placing the key in front of the cinema doors as if I'm stupid. 'We need to make sure Georgie knows the way back. There are things in this model that haven't materialised yet. She might get confused.' He glances sideways at me, suddenly serious. 'Look. She'll come out of these doors, once we've opened them, and walk around here, past the train station.' He traces the route with the tip of his finger. 'She takes a left onto the main street.'

'What if the witch follows her?'

'She'll have to run – down by these houses and out onto the mine track, then turn off for the water tank. When she gets to the tank, there'll be a hot-air balloon waiting to bring her home.'

'What about the witch?'

'Well, the balloon is by the water tank, right? So say the witch follows her. When Georgie gets to the tank, she'll wait until the witch is right beside her and then, quick as a wink, she'll push her in, jump into the balloon, and off she goes.'

'The witch drowns?'

'Shrivels up. Witches don't like water, remember?'

I start telling Georgie the plan. I sketch the whole thing out in my notebook, like a sort of map, to show her the way. She gets easily lost. And as you know, she can't read. I haven't told anyone about her leg. How can she run with a twisted leg? When I think of this, it makes me feel as if my skin has been turned inside out.

'She'll have plenty of stories to tell when she gets back, won't she?' Uncle Eddie says. 'You need some sleep.' When I lie back down on the settee, he adds, 'I ought to check what's going on. Will you be alright for a while?' He makes me drink some more water.

Then I think of something. 'Uncle Eddie, Georgie wants me to tell you that Dorothy doesn't get home in the hot-air balloon. The balloon takes off without her. She has to click her ruby slippers.'

'Does Georgie have any ruby slippers?'

'She has her red clogs but she's not wearing them.'

'Then she'll just have to catch the balloon.'

He taps me on the top of my head with his bunch of envelopes. 'I won't be long,' he says, waving the envelopes in the air as he leaves. 'Karlin's in the shop, if you need anything.' I can tell Uncle Eddie is frightened too. He doesn't say so, but I can tell. I keep my eye on the model of the cinema, waiting for Georgie to come out. Every so often she appears, and then she disappears. I don't get a chance to say goodbye.

EDDIE

On the way out, I ask Karlin to help herself to an ice-cream. She's leafing through the petrol coupons. Her blondish curls hide her eyes until she flicks her head back, rearranging her hair with a sweep of her hand. I watch her for a second. You couldn't call her beautiful, but she's strong, firm, and her skin is softer than it looks. I reckon she's about the same age as her predecessor – Shena Walker couldn't have been more than thirty, thirty-two perhaps. Shena was the second one to disappear.

'Moni's inside,' I say to Karlin, who nods, her face hardening as she turns away. At one time, I would have kissed her, before Caroline. I would have washed that hardness away.

The door judders behind me before the latch clicks in. I consider turning back. Maybe this isn't such a good idea. People might think I'm trying to hide something; they might ask questions. *Where is the money coming from?* Still, on balance, all things considered, what else can I do? A few hundred might be incentive enough for them to stay, buy me some time. *Sugar the old girl*, as my father used to say. The old man used to say a lot of things.

I slip my sunglasses on and tilt my hat forwards to stop the glare. It took me a while to get used to this climate, to the run of empty land. But one day I just knew. The whole country had climbed inside me overnight and there was no going back. Still, on days like this, you'd rather be anywhere else.

I don't take the truck, despite the heat. With all that's going on, I need to clear my head. Walking helps; it slows me down. So, the facts are, Georgie fell through a shaft and must have crawled her way along the tunnels. Once we scour the place properly – the detectives will bring dogs, they always do – we'll find her. She's underground, protected from the sun. It is possible she'll have nothing more than a few cuts and bruises. Why drag up the other two? Georgie hasn't disappeared.

I round the bend and approach the ghost gum tree, the one solitary tree in this town. Whatever else there was must have got knocked when they set up the first mine. The land was clear when we brought in the houses – twenty-six of them. Now of course there are only twenty-one, nine on the left and twelve on the right, including the bar and the general store. Still, it could be worse; I could have lost them all.

The white walls of the houses give off a glare. It's not hot, the day is only getting started, but this kind of light cuts right through you. Mr M's shadow stretches out under the tangle of branches, lying flat against the red dirt like a stain. Outback sun can play tricks on you, make you think you've lost your senses. I was up early one morning, months ago. Admittedly, I had a bit of drink inside me from the night before, but I could swear I saw that tree doing some kind of dance. The branches were moving. Don't get me wrong; I'm not into all this superstitious hoohaa some folk round here subscribe to. Cursed my arse. You'd want to hear the stories they cook up: snatching spirits or demons or God knows what.

In some ways, I blame Mr M. He sits under that tree all day, doing nothing – it makes people uneasy. I've tried to get him on his feet, offered him one of the mobile homes in exchange for a few hours manning the pumps. You'd think I'd asked him to paint the sky, the way he gawked at me. Mind you, he helped us out when Ted Hanson went missing. He knows this land backwards; every rock, every inch of arid bush. It's hard to imagine Akarula without him.

I stop just short of the tree and flick the brim of my hat. 'No doubt you've heard?' Mr M looks past me, and nods and breathes a little. I'm less put out by his silence than I used to be. 'They'll fish her out in no time.' I laugh, though it sounds more like a stutter.

'Them holes is what's causing all the trouble,' he says, stating the obvious. His face tightens as he thinks. I wait for more. There is no way of knowing whether the old man – not old so much as weathered – is done. Eventually I shake a finger at him and move on. He offers me his own finger flick. A man of few words, and yet the air is buzzing with him. He seems to stretch out beyond himself. I don't know what happened to the rest of his clan.

On reaching the first house, I post one of the envelopes through the door. A healthy cheque should do the job. Whatever people say, money can buy a man's mind, if not his soul. You don't choose to be an opal miner for the lifestyle. No, it's all about winning the jackpot, finding that magic stone. I understand the need for risk, for something more, something beyond the ordinary. I wrote the bloody book on it!

The women are marching across the scrub like a troop of sorry-arsed soldiers. It makes me sick, it really does. Georgie's out there; of course she is, but whether we find her or not is another question. When I first imagined this street, there were lamp posts down the centre, a green square in the middle, flags and bunting, the whole works. A cinema and dancehall were going to be where the service station is now. It's not a million miles from all that. Ok, it's just a street. The houses aren't as big, the patches of grass aren't as green as I would like, but it looks pretty good, considering.

I wave over at the women. They're still a fair way off – probably can't even see me. To do a search in this heat is no joke. These *Sheilas,* as they call them out here, are tough: elephant skinned, nothing gets through. At least it seems like that, until you get to know them.

Take the first search – we didn't think about going down the shafts for two days. It was Maddie – a good friend of Caroline's, Jake Brenton's wife – who figured out a system, two women holding the rope at the mouth of the shaft, another to climb down. That's heavy work. They painted a yellow x on each cap when they were done. I have to hand it to them; they were the last to give up. And when Shena Walker disappeared, they did it all over again, while the men carried on at the mine.

I stuff the envelopes in my shorts pocket and yank off my boot to shake out a stone: a red one the size of a tooth. Turning away from the women, I pull my boot back on. One day I'll have this road tarmaced as far as Wattle Creek. *The Akarula Highway.* It's not impossible.

It doesn't do to think too much about Georgie. Besides, the whole thing could be over in an hour or two. I might be regretting these cheques. But any longer than that and the risk of people leaving rises significantly. Empty houses mean repossession – that's the rule. There's no talking to the banks on that one, not anymore. No, this town needs people. The slightest whiff of more trouble is bound to send some of them awol, even though this is different. Monica saw Georgie. The child fell. She has not disappeared. I keep coming back to that one crucial fact.

Akarula and the rest of what you see is flat land. There are no hills to hide behind. But the ground is a bottomless pit. It all depends on how deep you're prepared to dig. The other two, the two who went missing, are out there somewhere; I'd stake my life on it.

Nine envelopes lighter, I cross to the other side of the street. No use rushing; we won't find her any quicker if I do. The squawking birds on the telegraph wire fill my head with noise, drowning out the rest. Maybe it's the shape they cut against the empty sky, or their constant chatter: either way, I get to thinking about those other buildings: the dome-fronted cinema, the high windows of the train station, the web of tarmac roads. One day this town will spread wide, the outskirts an hour's drive away, the scrubland pushed so far back that it touches the horizon. I can already see it.

Beyond the empty trailers and mobile homes on the left, two people, Mike and Caroline at a guess, are heading off down the mine track. They've been out since, what, five, six o'clock, wandering aimlessly; it's a blind man's game. I get the jitters just watching them. I can't help feeling that it's all too late.

Nevertheless, I kick on. I should have told Mike, course I should. I wanted too. Just couldn't seem to find the right moment. Once Georgie is found, there'll be no reason for people to leave. Even if she's dead. I can't think, I can't imagine, but still, even if she doesn't survive, it won't be anyone's fault. Accidents happen. Everyone understands that. I'm not one for praying, but if there is a God, he should bring her back alive, or else just bring her back. This town won't survive another mystery.

Of course, it won't be forgotten. You can't sweep something like this under the floorboards. Still, a sweetener should help. I slip an envelope into the general store. Ellie Warton outshines them all with her flower tubs. The bank took away the house next door, drove off with it on the back of an articulated lorry; a bit like pulling a tooth from the top set – the gap looks odd.

The whole street threatened to leave last year, and those living in the portacabins. People get unnerved when someone disappears. They think they might be next. I've thought about it myself, doing the disappearing trick, but then I get a flash of what this town could be – I see my model, or that damn tree – and, true as day, I can't let go. Mike needs this town as much as me. I promised him a decent place to live, and that's what he'll get. Whatever it takes.

The bar stands between two empty lots, its veranda marked with spit and ash, and the spill of last night's drink. I never drank much until I moved here; I mean I drank, but not like this. There's something sacred about the way the men, even the women, sit and study their drinks before knocking them back as if it were communion wine. I do it too, although probably not in the same way. The door is open, so I head inside and take a seat at the empty counter. Despite the hour, despite the fact, or because of the fact that my niece is six feet under or over or, God knows, somewhere sky high, I need a drink. I reach over to pull a beer from the hidden shelf on the other side. And then a head shoots up. I bolt backwards, almost losing my balance as I stretch out one foot to meet the floor.

'Did I frighten you?' Vera says, not quite smiling as she looks past me at the wall behind.

'Thought you'd be out with the rest,' I say.

Vera, ash-eyed thin-lipped Vera. She stuffs the flowery tea-towel she is holding into her back pocket and fetches up a bottle of beer, flipping the bronze top off like a pro. One thing I can say about Vera, she's the best barmaid in Western Australia. Face like the back end of a beer keg, but how and ever. We can't have everything.

'Any word?' She scrutinises the envelope I slip between the glass salt and pepper pots. 'What's this?'

'Bit of tax relief.' I start to unwind as the cold beer hits the back of my throat.

'I suppose those two detectives are on their way?' She slides a beer mat underneath my bottle. 'Bit early isn't it? How's Monica?'

'Fine.'

'What are they going to do?' She whips her tea-towel out again and bends down to retrieve one of the glasses she is drying off. Her skin is lined, marked with those brown spots old people have. She's not old, twenty, thirty something; only the way she moves her weight around and acts like everyone's grandmother puts years on her. Still, she can wet the mouths of fifty miners as quick as I can blink.

I peel back the corner of the label on the bottle.

'I don't know what I'd do if it were my child,' she says, holding up the glass to the dingy light. She spits on it and rubs a second time.

'She'll be alright. We found the cardigan.'

'I heard.'

'Any luck with that stone?'

Vera's face looks like it might slide off, but she says nothing. Her husband, Bill, lost a twelve pound opal last week. Reckons it fell out of his pocket on the way back from the mine, or else someone pilfered it. They've combed the track, searched the truck; no doubt Vera has scoured every inch of this bar. Cause everyone is saying it was an omen, Bill losing that stone. It could have set the pair of them up for life. Careless, if you ask me.

I take my time finishing the beer.

Vera turns to the back shelves and stacks the glasses. 'I wish Bill hadn't told me,' she says. 'Can't stop thinking about the damn thing.'

I chuck some money on the beer mat, throwing my bottle into the crate on the way out. At least Vera seems to be staying put. There's a good chance I'm overreacting. That said, I don't bother giving cheques to the mobile homes. There aren't many occupied, in any case. Most were vacated when Shena disappeared. I couldn't afford to pay everyone.

By the time the plane arrives – an eight-seater the same as last time – I'm almost at the service station. The airstrip, which peters out into a stretch of bush beyond the road's end, only becomes visible when there's a plane; the rest of the time it lies submerged in the scrub. As I watch the dust fly up and the wheels scream to a halt, I think of Monica and that hot-air balloon. There's a lot to be said for floating off into the blue.

Let me take you back, give you the whole picture. I moved to Australia close to six years ago, the end of 1979, not long after Dad died. Opportunities were ripe, and things in England weren't going too well. Mike was pretty low at the time, and what with Margaret Thatcher and the recession... I'd made a few contacts, an investment company that dealt mainly with overseas holiday lets. Wrote an impressive bio for myself as a property tycoon. It's amazing what people can swallow. Words on paper: that's what I tell Mike, and he's the wordsmith. I get this call from a mining company: Lansdowne Mining Corporation. All I had to do was reel them in.

I'll never forget that drive – the blinding heat, the red-chalk roads, those damn sticky flies. People say Akarula is like parts of Queensland, but it's not. Half of the cracks in the earth are wide enough to be craters. A moonscape is how my business partner, Willie Johnson, described it.

Our map took us as far as Wattle Creek. We stopped at a roadhouse, one of those wooden-walled establishments that remind me of the Wild West, stuffed animal heads staring out of the corners. Willie and I got steaks and talked to the local cowboys, who told us about a mine that had closed six months before. 'Nothing east of here,' one fella said. By the length of his hair and grey-brown beard, he might have been leaning up against that bar his whole life. 'This is the end of the road.'

He was right. From Wattle Creek the bitumen disappeared into dirt tracks. We followed the scant instructions Lansdowne Mining Corporation had sent us. Those tracks were rife with potholes. Where the tracks forked, we guessed at which one to take. Some of them petered out into impassable gullies. The further down those beaten tracks we went, the more geared up I got. I knew, even before we saw the place, that this was something big, the kind of opportunity that comes to you once in a lifetime.

Willie didn't share my enthusiasm. All he could see was no-man's land. Two miles or so before we reached the designated site, the Falcon overheated, blowing a gasket, and we were forced to walk, following a dried-out riverbed, one of the few features listed in our sparse directions.

It was as if the land had been blown apart and then scrambled back together. The whole place had a prehistoric feel. As we neared the site, we came across remnants of the old mine those cowboys had talked about – a few wooden shelters and derelict shacks, the odd burnt-out car – but nothing that suggested the makings of a town; just miles and miles of uninhabited bush, broken up by monolithic termite mounds, and one wide-armed tree. Willie reckoned the place had been abandoned in a hurry; none of the mineshafts were capped. We walked around the site, taking note of any geographical features that might hinder construction work. Lansdowne Corporation had already tested for water. It struck me as the perfect site.

Willie couldn't see it. I can hear him now. *Get the feeling we're in the forbidden zone?* He had this theory that anywhere more than fifty miles from civilisation was beyond the point of no return. *There are some places we're not meant to live. This looks like one of them.* I ignored him, totting up the countless advantages of establishing a town beyond the contours of the map. It was hard to imagine that there had ever been running water, yet there were gullies all over the place, and the riverbed, cracked and hardened by years of relentless sunshine, was fairly deep.

My brain was racing; I had a rush of ideas. Willie led the way up the side of a large red rock – the rock my nieces have christened Red Rock Mountain. The view from the top gave me the grand sweep of the place; in one blinding flash, I saw it all. My very own town. Something Dad would have been proud of.

'What shall we call it?' I asked Willie.

I knew he was assessing the potential, though he said nothing. What we needed were selling points, features that would attract miners. And Lansdowne Corporation had all that; the results of their initial explorations were impressive.

'There's my street, right there,' I said, pointing towards the riverbed. 'Two rows of houses to start with. Use the riverbed as the main road – plenty of room for expansion.'

Willie just shook his head. He didn't realise that what I had in mind was practically a city, a place that would be talked about, recognised on every map in years to come. I caught a glimpse of the infinite possibilities: a railway, a casino, a cinema. Right from the start I planned an eighty-seater cinema, for Mike. Once that was up and running, he wouldn't have to bother with his writing, which, as far as I could see, was making him pretty miserable.

I walked the whole site, checked out the old mine; it was perfect. On the way back, I found this boulder with the word *Akarula* scratched on it like some kind of stone-age graffiti. I wrote it down, even tried to find it in an Australian dictionary. It had a ring about it. That was good enough for me. (I never did find that boulder again.) By the time I got back to the car, Willie had managed to get it started.

The one-storey houses shot up in no time, leaving me four million in debt. Most of my borrowings were clean. I'd made the odd under-the-table deal, but who doesn't in this game? I'd built a town, the skin and bones of one, anyway. And I was the landowner, landlord, legal head. Some of them called me the bushmaster; it was more or less a standing joke. I knew there'd been trouble with a group of aborigines laying claims to the land, but I was well out of the line of fire. The mining company who had leased the mining rights before us, Opal Exports, were the ones facing the flak. I explained this to Willie. I wanted him to understand the long-term picture.

'Steer clear,' he kept saying, in that moralising tone of his. Within a month, he was gone.

I find Mike and Caroline in the sitting room. They look wrecked. Monica is asleep on the settee, which gives us all a good reason to stay quiet. Although eventually I say: 'The detectives have arrived.' I take a step closer to Caroline, who is standing in the middle of the room clutching something orange to her chest. Her eyes are glued to the certificate of land purchase framed on the wall behind me.

Mike has sunk down onto the arm of a chair and is holding his knees.

'You should rest,' I say, throwing my comment between them. Neither of them replies. The silence in the room could crush a cow, so I move back.

Before I reach the door, Mike says, 'Where have you been?' coiling his hands into his chest like a child. (It's the medication. He never used to be like this.)

'You need a drink,' I tell him. We all need a drink.

Mike shakes his head. 'Did you talk to the police?' He goes on in such a rush, his words bang into each other. And then he stops, glancing over at Monica, whose closed eyes are flickering. Her breath drones like a cat's purr.

'The detectives will be here any minute,' I say. 'What about some coffee?'

'What did you tell them?' Mike asks.

'They've only just landed. I haven't had a chance…'

I look back at Caroline, whose fingers are twitching, just her fingers; the rest of her is absolutely still. Her face has paled even more, and those fingers, they keep pawing at whatever she is holding.

Mike stands abruptly. His shirt flap is hanging out. He touches Caroline's arm as he goes past her. She grabs hold of his wrist, letting go of the orange knit; it's the cardigan we fished out from the shaft last night. As she bends to get it back, Mike frees himself from her grip and leaves. Only the questions he has asked take possession of the room like squatters.

When the door closes, Caroline finally speaks. 'Maddie says she's done this before.'

'That's right,' I say. It's hard to think straight; my mind keeps twisting up. I want to hold her, to feel the weight of her against me, only she's farther than the sea right now. Flat and lifeless in her near grief.

'What did she mean?' she says, cradling the cardigan in her arms.

The barking dogs are what wake Monica. I dive over to the settee, glad of something to do.

Monica wipes her lips with her finger end. 'The dogs are here,' she pipes, as if she is expecting them.

We all watch the door.

Mike is followed in by one of the detectives – Delaney. She's put on weight. Her short hair is slicked back, more likely with sweat than any hair product. In jeans and a well-worn shirt, she manages to look like an oversized circus attraction; she's a good foot taller than the rest of us. The large dark-haired mole on her cheek twitches as she gives me a cautious smile. I introduce her to Caroline.

The sight of this clownish woman unnerves me; if omens do exist, she must be one.

Monica gets up. 'Are those your dogs?'

Delaney nods, giving my niece a swift handshake before she moves on to Caroline.

'Georgie is trapped,' Monica says, causing Delaney to give her a perplexed squint of a look. Delaney has this odd way of stretching her lips over her buck teeth so that her mouth looks like a tightened fist.

'Trapped?'

'I gave her my cap. Do you think she's still wearing it? You're really tall.'

Caroline cuts in. 'Monica has been pretty sick with sunstroke, haven't you, pet? They were playing hide and seek...' She suddenly stops dead.

'Hide and seek,' Delaney repeats in a mechanical way that strips the words of any meaning. Then she turns to me. 'How long has the child been missing?'

Mike butts in before I can answer. 'Yesterday evening. I found Moni about six o'clock.' He runs on with other details that Delaney picks through. When he is done, she flicks her tongue over her top teeth. 'Let's get going while we have the light. We'll need something with her smell on it, anything she would have worn recently.'

Caroline holds out the orange cardigan: the same sunburnt orange as the car I used to drive.

'For the dogs,' Delaney explains, once we are outside. She passes the cardigan to her partner, Walsh, who is waiting beside

51

the tethered Alsatians. Despite Walsh's vain attempts to fan himself with a sheet of paper, his face is flushed. He is wearing the same dark suit and baseball cap that he wore last time.

'Mr Harvey,' he says, stowing the paper into his trouser pocket. He offers me his freed hand, which he withdraws before I manage to reach him. The backs of his hands are raw with some kind of eczema. I noticed this the last time, though today the condition seems worse.

Monica almost bowls Walsh over. 'Are these yours?' she asks, petting the dogs furiously, forcing her way in between them. 'Our dog was called Trim. We buried him under the crab apple tree. What's this one called?'

'Alice Two. This one is Darwin, and that's Alice, named after their birthplaces.'

The dogs' leads are attached to the outside tap.

'Hello, Alice.'

Walsh and Monica ramble on like this while Delaney talks us through the procedure. With her usual curtness, she makes no promises, instructing us as if this were a military drill. She would have suited the army. Her voice alone gives me a firearm prod in the stomach. I know that we are on the same road as last time; there's no escape – even if it does turn out differently.

It's decided that once we reach the shaft, we'll split up. Caroline will follow the detectives westwards; Mike and I will head east. The women are already raking the ground south of the mine. In an hour or two we should be back, and with any luck, can put the whole thing behind us. Somehow I'll persuade Mike not to leave. The cinema projector should be here in a week or two.

Caroline orders Monica back inside. 'Don't go anywhere.'

She gives me a fleeting glance as her eyes swing between Monica and the shop door. Those eyes. Caroline is not like any other woman; there is something wild about her – a fire. You should hear her voice: like blue cheese and velvet twisted together. She's impossible to make sense of, changes all the time. You'd never get bored with a woman like that.

'I know where Georgie is,' Monica announces.

'Where?' Walsh likes my niece. He probably has children of his own.

'She's trapped. Someone locked the door.'

Caroline interrupts: 'Do as you're told.'

But Walsh keeps asking questions. Monica tips her head sideways as she tells him everything. After a brief consultation with Delaney, Walsh addresses Caroline and Mike. 'Children often have a better instinct for finding people ... if you don't mind her coming?'

Since neither of them reacts, Walsh winks at Monica, handing her one of the dog's leads. The six of us cross the road and strike out towards the old mine. With no wind, our tracks could stay for weeks, months; you can always tell where people have been. Mr M knows whose footprints belong to whom; he has a gift, apparently. He can even tell what mood a person was in: did they stamp, did they skip, that sort of thing. But when there are no footprints...

Delaney channels her energies into Mike. 'You said you last saw your daughter around nine or ten yesterday morning.'

'She and Monica were playing behind the caravan.' Mike searches the backs of his hands before shoving them into his pockets.

'And you don't know what she was doing after that?' There is a hint of criticism in Delaney's tone. She starts whistling some annoying repetitive tune, interrupting herself to say: 'People go missing all the time. We've got a list a mile long. Some people want to disappear: start a new life, shed their old skin. With children it's obviously different. In most cases they just wander off and get lost. Those dogs should be able to sniff her out pretty quickly. If she's down there.' This is Delaney's idea of small talk. Thankfully she doesn't mention the other two. Mike should find out from me.

'Where else would she be?' Caroline asks, although she is not really asking.

Delaney pauses. 'It's always better not to assume too much.' The moment she cracks her knuckles, the conversation is over.

We use the service station and Red Rock Mountain as base points to check how far we've come. Although it was dark when we found the shaft last night, I can more or less gauge the distance. When we find the spot, Delaney gets down on her hunkers and examines the stones around the opening.

'She hasn't got her clogs on,' Caroline says. 'I can't get her to wear them. We got them specially made; they're probably not that comfortable.' There is a metal coating to her voice which makes her sound like someone else. These situations, the stress of them – people change; I've seen it before. God knows, I wish I hadn't.

Delaney lets Caroline witter on while she presses her lips tightly together, giving the impression of mild concern. 'Righto,' Delaney says, peering into the dust. We all peer into the dust.

Walsh makes a few notes and then asks Monica, 'When you talked to your sister, did she say anything?'

'Her leg was crooked, like this.' She cocks out her own leg, twisting it backwards. 'There's not much room down there.'

'It's important that you try to remember as much as you can,' Walsh says, squatting down next to Monica. She nods solemnly, but says nothing more, studying her now straightened leg.

I map the tunnels that lead off the shaft, scratching out dirt lines with my foot. 'We've been down all three,' I say, redefining the third line. 'Nothing.'

'What's Georgina like at climbing?' Walsh asks.

'She's four,' Mike says. 'That's a sheer drop.'

Monica stares fixedly at Walsh. 'If you were playing hide and seek, where would you hide?' Before he has a chance to answer, she says, 'There is nowhere to hide, is there?'

She's right. There is nowhere to hide.

After the detectives have finished their inspection of the shaft and asked me and Mike another few questions, we separate, making a slight adjustment to the plan. Mike and Monica go west, the two detectives and Caroline fan out east with the dogs, and I head north. I walk from shaft to shaft, hauling off the wooden caps and hollering Georgie's name. The echo fires back at me. GEORGIE! GEORGIE! GEORGIE! Now and again I stop to listen, straining for a trace of her voice. Sometimes I think I hear her amongst the shickering of insects and the rish rish of dry scrub. Georgie is a real charmer; her feathery sparrow voice always makes me smile.

There must be a nine or ten-mile radius to this old mine. I remember Willie asking, *why do you think the last miners left in such a hurry?* I don't think he knew the answer himself, although he made out he had a fair idea. I actually don't care why they left. People come and go. That's life. Not everything has to be a damn drama. Willie had his mind set against Akarula from the beginning. He's one of those characters who believe he's always right.

GEORGIE! GEORGIE! GEORGIE! I make sure I secure each cap before pushing on to the next. I could sue the clowns who sold these caps; rotten, every last one of them. Another cut and run company out to make a fast buck. No one seems to care anymore. Mike, on the other hand, would give you his arms and legs if you needed them. He doesn't deserve this. None of us deserves this.

The sky flattens into a blue heat as I carry on, slowly; it's difficult to orientate with everything shimmering. Then Monica's scream rips through the bush-drone. I don't think what it might mean at first. It takes me a while to locate the direction of the sound. When I spot her and Mike, I start to run. It's not easy; the rough ground makes speed impossible. I have to weave between wire tufts of scrub grass and small boulders. As I approach them, it dawns on me that Georgie must be dead. They must have found her body. Maybe they've found one of the other bodies. What if all three are in the same place? I'd let go of believing we would actually find them. I thought it was going to be some life-long mystery. But once we have bodies, Delaney and Walsh can nail the culprit. If we have a murderer, the town's reputation could be saved. Even if we don't, at least the superstitions and wild ghost rumours can stop. One woman, weeks after Ted Hanson disappeared, swore she saw him walking down the street. I reckon that's what she wanted to see. Like I said before, this outback sun plays tricks.

I stop short of Monica and Mike, taking a moment to catch my breath. You wouldn't believe the things that flash through my mind in the next few seconds. All the horror films I've ever seen rolled into one. I flip a coin in my pocket for a few seconds before I cross the last stretch of scrub. I'm sweating like a spit-fired pig. It's not the heat; it's the pressure that makes my skin drip.

Monica is shaking violently, pressing her hands to her head, really distraught. I'm ready for the worst. Mike tries to calm her down; he clamps his arms around her waist. When I reach them, he signals over to a big clump of scrub grass. All I see at first is the scrub grass. Then I walk around to the other side and there it is, destroyed by flies, open picking for the birds, but still recognisable. My stomach does a U-turn.

'It's a joey!' I'm so relieved, I burst out laughing. 'My god, you had me going then. Calm down, Monica. It's only a baby kangaroo.'

She is not the least bit consoled.

Mike more or less spits at me. 'I'll take her back. Tell the others what happened.'

When he starts to lead Monica away, she breaks free of him and shoots across to the corpse. She plunges to the ground and stretches out beside it, running her hands along the length of its mangy body.

'Don't touch it!' Mike shouts.

But she presses her head against the animal's open belly. He has to prise her off. Children can be pretty morbid. Mike was the worst; he was always cutting up animals to get a look at their insides.

He leads Monica off, though she keeps pulling back. He has to carry her in the end. She'll be a real stunner when she's older; the same wavy auburn hair as Caroline. I'm so relieved, I actually cry; I cry in the midst of shaking laugher, no doubt owing to lack of sleep.

Systematically, I make my way between each shaft, pulling off the caps, calling down, until the sun disappears. It feels good to be on my own, mostly; now and again I get a bit spooked at the idea of being out here with God knows what on the loose. I know exactly what we're in for. The interviews will start. People will cook up fantastical explanations guaranteed to fuel mass panic. And I'll have to create new tactics to calm the storm. It's like the worst recurring dream. On top of which, it is Georgie.

When I get back to the service station, I wait by the pumps for a while, watching the moon grow in the darkening sky. Nothing will be the same after this. There is no going back to those early days. In four years this town has developed a hunch, and grown as rough as toad skin. We all have.

I'll tell you what I see when I close my eyes; I see this street with its identical houses and pinched together gardens, children climbing lampposts and flying flags that turn into butterfly wings. It's my street. I'm walking up and down, watering the houses as if they were flowers, lifting off the roofs to watch the people inside. My street. I wish Dad was alive to see what I have done.

When I open the sitting-room door, Caroline shoots towards me, stopping mid-stride to look at Monica, who is writhing on the settee, her face wet with sweat. We both watch her until Caroline says, 'I thought you were the doctor.'

There is so much I could say, so much I want to say, but none of it seems relevant. And so I draw her into the next room where we can be alone. I lift her face towards mine and kiss the tears that roll down her cheeks. Then I unbutton the front of her dress. Just as my mouth reaches her breast, she pulls away.

Mike is studying a map of the old mine, which is pinned to the kitchen wall. It must be close to dawn. He makes pencil marks where we've already searched. Without looking back at me, he asks, 'Who's Ted Hanson?' The relief, at first, is overwhelming. I can feel the push of it all, like a giant wave, as I get ready to rush the whole thing out. I never meant to hide what happened. As I said, the timing wasn't right.

I drop into a chair at the kitchen table and search the map for a starting point. It's hard to find the right road in. Mike turns around, clutching at his arm below the elbow with his other hand, his shoulders slumped in their usual position. So I begin. 'Two years ago Ted went missing. It was a Wednesday.

He turned up at the mine, left work, and then vanished somewhere between the drop-off point and the street. The men came over the next evening. He hadn't showed and wasn't at home. They thought he might be with me.' I have imagined having this conversation, what I would say, how Mike would react. It wasn't like this. We were in the bar, for a start. The whole thing was more of a sideways comment than an actual conversation: a point of interest, a snippet of information, something Mike could write about if he wanted to. Mike moulds his face into a chipped expression I can't make out, and because he stays silent, I go on.

'We searched everywhere, went through all the shafts twice, three times, kept thinking we'd missed something. No one leaves this town without being seen. There is only one way out by road, and his car was still here. We'd had no planes, no one driving in or out.'

'What did the police say?'

'They wrote a missing person's report. We thought he'd turn up. It wasn't like he was dead.'

'Did he take clothes? Food?' Mike is growing agitated; his neck is a patchwork of reds. 'What about friends, relatives?'

'Nothing. He wasn't married.'

'You're not married. Would you just up and leave without telling anyone?'

'Look, Mike, I don't know. It's a different world out here. People get crazy. Maybe he just couldn't hack it and skidaddled. Haven't you ever wanted to disappear?'

Mike stares at me for what feels like a long time, and then he says: 'We're at least a hundred miles from anywhere. Anyone who tried to leave on foot would die of heat exhaustion if nothing else got them first. People don't just disappear.'

'I would have told you eventually. You had enough on your

plate. Anyway, we know Georgie fell down a shaft. Let's not mix things up.'

'Why haven't we found her?' He steps forward and grabs the back of the nearest chair. 'She's not the kind of child to go racing through underground tunnels. Moni said her leg was hurt. She couldn't have gone that far. We've looked within at least a five-mile radius. Where the hell is she?'

I take a steady breath before I say: 'Ted's not the only one.'

By the blankness on Mike's face, he seems not to have understood. So I explain. 'Last year a woman went missing: Shena Walker. Last February. Everyone knew her husband was knocking her about. She'd probably had enough. Only we couldn't figure out how she'd left. Unless she'd hitched a ride with the food truck or the mail plane. I checked both. Denis – you know Denis, our pilot from Wattle Creek – he was in Sydney at the time, so there was no other way out. She didn't take the car, obviously.' Mike puts his hand over his mouth and lets it slide down his chin, and then he brings his fingers back up to his lips. I can't tell if he is mad or just undone. 'We thought she'd turn up….'

I go on to tell him everything. Well, nearly everything. I leave out the fact that Shena Walker used to clean this house, once a week, on a Friday. She went missing on a Friday. I must have known before anyone else. When she didn't turn up for work, I called down to her house. She'd left the radio on. I knew something was wrong. She wasn't just my cleaning lady; we fooled around – nothing serious, not like Caroline.

I wasn't surprised when her husband arrived the next day. I told him she'd been to clean the house and left at four o'clock as usual. Don't ask me why I lied. Once I'd said it, there was no going back. I didn't want another mystery on my hands, so I carried on as if everything was normal. I kept leaving her envelopes underneath the counter in the shop each Friday, hoping she'd turn up. When her husband left, two weeks later, I gave him all the money. Within a month the bank had repossessed the house.

Mike is shouting. 'Do you think we'd have let the girls roam around like that if we'd have known? Georgie's four. What chance has she got?'

'Calm down.'

'Calm down?'

I understand why he's angry, of course I do, but Mike has never been able to see the bigger picture; he always gets twisted up in some detail.

'I wanted to tell you when I was over last year, but we were having such a good time, and I just needed to forget the whole thing. I thought the fuss might blow over. And then I finally got you here. I didn't want you turning round and going home.'

Mike puts one of his hands on the top of his head and looks down. When he looks up again, his lips are slightly parted as if he's about to speak. I wait, winding the loose button thread on my shirt around my finger. I pluck at the thread a bit, and then go to the fridge for two beers, one of which I set down in front of him. I pull the damn thread some more as I say: 'I'm sorry, Mike. I really thought it was all over.'

I flip the beer top and take a swig, throwing the opener down beside his bottle. For a few seconds I glimpse the stubborn fiery bastard Mike used to be, the way his face sets hard.

'What are we supposed to do?' he asks.

'We keep looking. I'll see to it those shafts are properly sealed off as soon as we find her. I'll get a fence put up.'

'A fence?' Mike moves around the table towards me. His face is bright red. 'A fence?' he repeats.

'Where are you going?'

He bolts out. I give the shirt thread a final tug and my button falls to the floor.

Susan doesn't comment on the beer in my hand. She drops her doctor's bag so that she can hug me properly.

'Don't suppose they've found her then?' is what she says. 'Caroline called. Where are they?' She steps back to take a good look at me. I haven't showered or shaved in two days. 'What did they say about the others?' She waits for my response. When nothing comes, she says, 'You *have* told them?'

I nod, directing her towards the sitting room.

Susan is the only person who understands that none of this is my fault. I can still hear Mike, the outrage, as if I'd somehow betrayed him. I haven't betrayed anyone. All the same, I know I made a mistake, but things can still turn around.

Let me tell you a story about my older brother. When he left university, he was the brightest of the bunch, a real star. (I was never much of a scholar.) Mike met Caroline that same year, in Paris I think. She was doing some student exchange, singing in a jazz bar at night. I didn't like her at first. Found her a bit thin, not literally, but she didn't have much zazz. It was only after she had Monica that her singing really took off. She grew on me. I hung around their house in Hendon quite a lot; I had nowhere of my own at the time.

A friend of mine working on the stock exchange gave me a few tips. After a couple of failed attempts, I struck lucky; that was really what set me up. But Mike, he always worked like a dog and kept his head down, just like Dad. Never complained, never asked for anything. *You reap what you sow, and what you don't sow won't grow.* What I envied Mike was that he seemed satisfied. I tried to show him that there was more to life, but in a way he had it all. And I had nothing: money, yes, women galore, but nothing worth dying for.

After Mike had the car accident – he didn't even hit the child – he stopped driving and sort of curled up in a ball. I was amazed. I couldn't believe that the great Mike had fallen flat. I tried everything I could, but he wouldn't shake himself out of it. Next thing, he's working in some back street cinema doing bitty reviews for the local press. I suppose what I'm trying to say is, even the best of us can miss a pitch.

When I get to the sitting room, Monica is asleep again. Caroline and Susan are deep in discussion with Maddie Brenton, a blunt decent woman – knows a nail from a screw. The three of them are clustered together by the window like witches. They stop talking when they see me.

'Is she alright?' I ask. From their rolled-up faces I can tell they don't know who I'm talking about. 'Monica – is she alright?'

Susan nods and picks up her bag: 'She'll have to sleep here for a while. The caravan will be too hot. Keep the air-conditioning on. You know where I am.' She takes leave of the women and smiles briefly as she walks past me. Caroline doesn't look at me as she follows Susan through to the shop.

I drag the camp bed out from under the cabinet. Maddie helps me lift it over to the wall, by the window. 'Michael's still out, I take it?' I say.

She doesn't answer, just undoes the clip and flips the mattress down. Maddie is broad, big-chested, with a set of biceps that puts me to shame, but she is straight as they come – says what she means. I like that. We arrange the sheets and then I lift Monica off the settee and lay her down carefully on the camp bed. Her breath quickens but she doesn't wake.

'Thank god for sleep,' Maddie says, staring at Monica with a tired look on her face. 'We've been trying to work out what the connection between the three of them might be. You any ideas, Mr Harvey?' (She insists on calling me Mr Harvey.) 'Ted was a pretty happy-go-lucky sort of fella, not an obvious target for anyone. Then Shena. I didn't realise she was pregnant.'

'Pregnant?' I get this sickening feeling, a hot-cold flush that traps the air inside me. I stare out of the window while Maddie goes on.

'Imagine, she's up the duff and there he is, pounding her. Good job he moved out. Sick bastard.'

I offer Maddie a beer, which she accepts, knocking the top off on the edge of the windowsill. 'And now little Georgie, not the brightest button in the box. What do you make of it? The only thing the three of them have in common, as far as I can see, is that they live in this shithole. No offence.' Maddie downs her beer in large gulps. 'Jake says the men are knocking off early to help with the search.'

'Good.' I breathe deliberately in an effort to keep my balance.

Maddie slaps my shoulder as she goes out. I watch Monica sleep for a while. With my left hand on the sheet I try to smooth out the creases.

Walsh and Delaney call over around eight o'clock the next evening. I lead them into the office. There's a faint whiff of perfume in the air, Caroline's; it isn't a flowery smell, more like wood after rain. Makes me feel oddly nostalgic.

Pulling out a couple of chairs, I offer our guest detectives a drink, but it seems that I'm the only one in need of refreshment. So I pour myself a whiskey, taking a swig before I sit. My desk is cluttered. Monica used to sort my papers into neat piles before all this rigmarole. Walsh asks after my eldest niece as he strides around the room, finally standing behind Delaney's chair.

'The doc gave her a tranquilliser,' I tell him.

He nods and then shakes his head.

'We need a few more details from you,' Delaney says, dragging her chair up to my desk.

'Fire away.'

'What is Georgina's middle name?'

'Her middle name?'

'You are her uncle?'

If I smoked, I'd light a cigarette right now. Since I don't, I pick at my left nostril and study Delaney's teeth.

It's a good minute before she goes on: 'How would you describe your relationship with your niece?'

'My relationship?'

She throws a sharp glance back at Walsh, which stops him from flicking his pen on and off.

'In the average day,' she says, forcing her words through those enormous teeth, 'how much time did you spend with Georgina? On average.'

I make one of those huffing sighs. Can't help myself. 'She takes a bath every day. Cleanest girl I ever met.' No one laughs. 'It's an obsession.'

'An obsession?'

'The caravan doesn't have a bath.'

Delaney finally cuts to the kernel. 'What's your theory, Mr Harvey?' She drops her clasped hands on the desk and leans in towards me.

'My theory is that Georgie fell down a shaft.'

'If it wasn't for the fact that she has water – am I right in thinking she has some kind of water bottle?' I nod. 'If it wasn't for that, there is no way she would survive. Four days is a long time. Even with water, it's unlikely.'

'Unlikely.'

'How do you explain the fact that she hasn't been found? That none of the three missing have been found?' She sits back, taking her hands off the desk.

'I'm not the detective,' I say. Delaney has a way of winding me up, making me come out with all these smart comments.

Walsh starts pacing, tapping his pen against his forehead. We both watch him. When he stops tapping, Delaney turns back to me. 'Would you say that you and Georgina were close?'

'Did you ever keep goldfish?' Before Delaney jumps in, I add: 'Georgie's a bit like a goldfish. Goes round and round without bothering. Doesn't care whether she passes a bridge or one of those fake castles. Fish don't mind if you buy coloured stones or grey stones for the bottom of the tank.'

'I don't think… '

'You asked if we are close. As close as you get to your goldfish that you feed every day. You don't want it to die.'

As she gets up, I ask: 'Do you think the other two were murdered?' It's a valid question.

'Do *you*?' Delaney gives me her interrogator's eyes. I might as well be in a James Bond film, except my office lacks the wall-sized fish tank and the requisite blonde. (Delaney is mouse-brown and as far from a Bond girl as … well, you or I.)

Enough's enough. 'Sleep well,' I say, heading for the door. 'Be a long day tomorrow.'

Delaney nods in her trite, contradictory way. I open the door and see them both out through the sitting room. Monica is balanced on the edge of the settee, writing in her notebook. I'm surprised she's still awake.

Walsh peers over her shoulder. 'Busy, eh?'

'You haven't found her, have you?'

Unfazed by Monica's directness, he says: 'Not yet.' He frowns slightly, picking at the flaking skin on his fingers.

'She's good at hiding, isn't she? Better than me.'

He pushes out a smile and follows us into the hall, closing the door behind him. In a low voice he asks: 'What do you know about Mr M?'

'As much as you. I told you everything last time, there isn't much to know.'

They leave. The slap of the door closing makes the air sting red for a second or two. In the dim of the shop nightlights I notice that the canned drinks need restocking. Another job for Karlin tomorrow. I don't tell her what to do; she's her own boss. Only sometimes I notice things.

I stay out of the search. Someone has to keep an eye on Monica. By 9 am I'm in the office making calls to fencing contractors, trying to get the best deal. I fix an appointment with Barrier Lines. Then I go through some paperwork, spin another story to the bank, write to my lawyer friend. This way I get through the morning without stewing too much. In my experience, once you let yourself believe the worst, it might as well have happened.

Caroline comes in around lunchtime to check on Monica.

'Any luck?' I ask. I lean back against the office door, holding a mug of tea.

She props herself on the edge of the camp bed, smoothes the hair off Monica's face, and starts talking in a whisper.

'Do you need anything?' I say. She pulls the sheet up to Monica's chin and adjusts the cover. 'Caroline?'

After a minute or so she gets up and leaves without acknowledging me. That's when I slam the mug hard against the wall. It smashes; shards of porcelain and lukewarm tea fly across the room. Monica hides her head under the sheet. After hammering out my full range of curses, I decide to follow Caroline, but change my mind as I reach the door.

'Uncle Eddie?' Monica emerges from the sheet and hoists herself up on her elbow. 'Are you cross with me?'

'Course not. Sorry, skunk. Didn't mean to frighten you.' I pick up the bigger pieces of mug and chuck them in the bin.

Mug-throwing is not the kind of thing I would normally do. 'Things don't always work out the way you want them to.'

'What do you think Georgie is doing?' Monica knits her hands together and stares at me.

I want to give her an answer, something that might make her smile, but the best I can come up with is: 'I don't know. I really don't.'

Monica nods. 'She's got us this time.'

A week goes by. Let me take you through it. Last Tuesday, the day Caroline ignores me, I drink a bottle of wine and add three new buildings to my Akarula model. The next day, mid-morning, Caroline marches in. I'm in the office doing paperwork. She stands in front of my desk, arms folded, and says, 'Seeing as you're not bothering, can you at least watch Moni.' Not bothering? What's that supposed to mean? She doesn't give me a chance to ask or explain, just rushes out as if she's being chased. What difference will an hour make? Mid-morning is our time. Ordinarily Mike would still be asleep.

Thursday, Caroline and Mike come in exhausted. I've made dinner, which neither of them eat. Mike plays around with his cutlery. When I turn on the light – we've been sitting in the dark – Mike says, 'I don't believe…' and stops right there, looking down at his knife as if he's never seen one before. Then he sinks into his half-sleep state. Caroline flaps around, fetching water for his bloody pills, but then he springs to life. 'I'm going back out.' He lets his knife fall to the floor.

'There's no point searching in the dark,' I tell him as he does up the laces on his boots.

Caroline tacks on behind him, turning to say, 'He won't sleep until he finds her.'

So Mike is suddenly the hero; and the way Caroline's been looking at me lately, I must be the Anti-Christ. If I worked like a dog, would that make me a better person? Is it a sin to live the easy life? No life is easy. Surely she knows that. There are people searching; detectives on the job. Why not let them get on with it? She's furious with me for not beating myself into the ground like her and Mike. I know she is, but she doesn't realise that I'm already ten feet under.

Well that was Thursday. Then Friday I meet her in the shop, just as I'm leaving to go and check some details for the fencing contractor who is due to arrive any day. We hover either side of the crisp stand. Caroline asks where I'm going. When I tell her, she shakes her head in disbelief. I understand that she's distraught, but why take it out on me? Can't she see what I'm doing? Doesn't she get the fact that I am trying to protect everyone?

'What's happened to you, Eddie?'

Frankly I wasn't going to get into one of her brain-wrecking conversations, so I left it at that.

Saturday comes and goes. I don't see Caroline at all; she basically avoids me. Sunday, she is out all day, searching with the rest of them. I check up on Monica every now and then, but I've got work to do. And she seems fine. She's an independent sort of girl.

Mike comes in around lunchtime with a small plastic figure in his hand, which is hard to see because it's caked in dirt. He shows it to Monica, who just shrugs and goes back to her book. I ask him what he's doing.

'Thought it might have been Georgie's. I found it behind one of the portacabins,' he says, wiping it clean with his shirt flap. When he leaves, I throw the figure in the bin. Does he really think this will help?

Mike spends most of Monday with the detectives, and I figure that if I'm going to make it up with Caroline, now is my chance. We're in the kitchen. I rustle Monica onto her feet, and ask Caroline if she wants to come for a drive.

'A drive?' she says, acting all furious again before storming out and forgetting her sun hat.

My niece and I drive round to the general store, which is more or less in the middle of the street. Monica shoots off down the side of the wall to fetch the watering can. Ellie Warton may have given up with the lawn, but the tubs are a blaze of colour: some sort of thick-leafed ivy, and a succulent with reddish leaves that Michael calls Devil's Tail.

'Post arrived?' I ask as I go in. The store is like a cave, with metal shelves stacked up to the ceiling. Ellie is piling bags of sugar in a pyramid on the counter. She's the kind of woman you can imagine baking bread in the middle of a typhoon.

'Well?' she says, with her customary sigh. She is the oldest of the Akarula women, fifty-something at a guess. Her husband, Scott, has been a miner, or at least involved in mining, for over thirty years.

'I thought I heard the mail plane.'

'About an hour ago. I expect this is what you're looking for.' There are a pile of letters and small packages on the counter, but then I see the box on the floor behind her. Ellie plucks at the dark hairs on her chin as she studies me.

'They said it was a big one.' I go round and try to lift it, but can't shift the thing more than an inch.

'Weight of a dead body,' she says without smiling.

I push the box outside.

'Wait up.' Ellie goes through to the back and comes out wheeling a trolley. Together we manage to lug the box onto the metal prongs. Can't say I especially like this woman. Her eyes are too small; they make her look mean. Both of us watch Monica spray the flowers with that red tin watering can.

'How's Scott getting on?' I wheel the box over to the truck with Ellie bent over holding on to the front.

'Asthma's at him.' She runs her hand down the side of the box and then pins me with one of her small-eyed stares. 'How old is she?'

'Four.'

She nods and shifts round to Monica. 'Aren't you the best helper? Wait up till I see what I can find.'

Monica is not stupid. Every time she waters Ellie's tubs, she gets a free notebook.

'What's in the box?' Monica asks as we drive back.

'A surprise for your dad.'

At the service station, I pull up outside the shed, and push the box in with Monica's help. Mike's birthday is not for another week.

And now it's Tuesday again. A handful of people have already turned up to complain about their bounced cheques. I explain that there has been a miscommunication and assure them that I will sort it out. I'm on a thin rope, though. Any day now the bank will send their house-thieves in to repossess the lot, unless I can convince them to stay. People are restless. My fence should be up in a week, which will lend some security to the place. It doesn't help that Delaney and her sidekick are going round like a pair of scaremongers. They've already stayed too long. The last time it was only three days.

It's not that I don't want to believe in this searching business. I don't want to put a damper on their efforts, but between you and me, what are the chances? How many days is it now? Twelve, and no sign. She could turn up – I'm not saying she won't – but you have to admit that it's unlikely. All we can reasonably hope for is to find a few bones.

It's not clear who exactly calls the meeting on Wednesday night. I get word from Maddie, who has heard from Vera. Vera tells us it will be in the back room of the bar. We congregate around 8 pm. The pool table has been pushed to one side and the chairs are arranged in a horseshoe in the centre. There are notable absences: Delaney and Walsh, Mike, who has stayed to see to Monica, and Mr M. Caroline sits next to Maddie. I stand at the back, by the open door, prepared for a quick exit. The time for rousing speeches encouraging them all to stick together, to stay put, has come and gone. Maddie's husband, Jake, speaks first, addressing everyone from the front.

'We all know why we're here.' There are a few nods and murmurs of agreement, but most of us wait for him to carry on. 'We've searched the entire area. Every man in this room was at the mine on the day Georgina disappeared.' I consider pitching in at this point, but what's the use. 'Vera can account for most of the women. Someone somewhere knows where that girl is. It's about time we got some answers.'

There is a smattering of applause, but the general mood is cautious. Scott Warton, a butcher of a man with age against him, gets up.

'I hear what you're saying, Jake, but we can't go taking the law into our own hands. I say let the police deal with him.' He wheezes. Vera passes him a glass of water.

Jake retorts, 'They've had two years.'

I can feel the temperature rising. I've heard all the sacred ground skin and bone stories, the sorcery hair-burning crap, but I wasn't expecting this. I'm halfway through the door when Caroline's voice stops me. She is standing in the centre of the room.

'I am going to find my daughter. She is out there somewhere.' There is a respectful silence as she walks through the crowd, right past me.

I go after her. 'I don't know what the hell that was about,' I say. She keeps walking. 'What are they going to do? *Taking the law into our own hands.*' I'm not expecting her to speak; that's why I rattle on. I just want to be near her.

She stops when we reach the last house before the bend, and turns to face me. 'Do you realise that we were having sex when Georgie went missing? I was with you instead of looking after my daughter. I was with *you*. And now I'm being punished. I deserve to be punished.' Her face splinters; she cries loudly as her body crumples over. I catch her with both hands before she hits the ground. All I can do is hold onto her. 'I was with you,' she keeps repeating as she cries. Maybe she's right, maybe this is some kind of punishment. But hearing her voice, feeling her breath against my chest, makes everything seem alright.

Day fourteen. I'm in the shop totting up the figures from the day before, waiting for the fencing contractor to arrive. He promised to come last Thursday. If this firm wasn't the cheapest, I'd have gone elsewhere. I'm bound to lose one or two houses, I know that. Like last time. If people understood that leaving their houses will result in the bank taking them, maybe they'd stay? Nobody wants to see a town disappear.

They are still looking – the women, Mike, Caroline. The men have gone back to work. Mike has figured out that if Georgie sips 12 ml of water per day, she could survive for up to three weeks, even more. It all depends on how full that bottle was in the first place. No one has bothered to point out that a four year old is unlikely to make such calculations, and what about food?

A Barrier Lines truck pulls up outside. The rep sidles in, chewing gum. Not a good start, as far as I'm concerned.

'Harry Redman from Barrier Lines.' The young fella shakes my hand vigorously, a bright-eyed, sun-tanned type with ragged golden locks. No doubt dances a rare tune with the ladies. 'I've got the fastest team in the business,' he says.

'I want the best team in the business.'

'Yes, sir.' He makes me feel like an old man with his jaunty attitude and his gum. I fetch the plans from the office and spread them out on the counter, circling the whole area, including the patch that used to be mined by Opal Exports.

'You want the fence to go around the town?' he asks, despite my having just illustrated as much. 'Afraid of a roo invasion?'

'Can you do it?' I say dryly. His laugh irritates me; the shine off his oversized forehead irritates me. I can smell his sweat-drenched skin.

He nods and writes down the price. 'We'd like half upfront. Company policy.'

Smarter than I thought. I write a cheque. That buys me three, four days. By then the fence will be up, according to his estimate. We can renegotiate later. This was Willie's end of the business. He would put the thumbscrews on and get the price right down, tell them he'd found a better deal. I did try getting Willie back, offered to double his salary, but he was adamant. *That place gave me the heebegeebees* is what he said.

The Barrier Lines rep turns out to be a curious soul. 'What's with this place, anyway?' I rip out the cheque and hand it over. 'They found that girl yet?'

'You and your men best get started then.'

He folds the cheque, pinching the crease between his fingers before tucking it into his shirt pocket. Smug git.

I sit on the stool behind the counter, staring at the plans for the fence. You've always got to factor in some additional costs. With this fence, it's the principle of the thing that matters, like having an alarm box outside a house; it acts as a deterrent, gives a feeling of security. That's what counts.

Mike creeps in so quietly I don't notice him until he drops his bag down on the other side of the counter.

'I'm taking Moni to the hospital for tests. The fevers are getting worse. We'll be back first thing in the morning. Keep an eye on Caroline.' I think of telling him he looks like a shipwreck, but what's the point?

'What do you think of this?' I follow the pencil-lined fence with my fingertip.

Mike stares at the map for a second. 'Did you hear what I just said?'

'She's in safe hands,' I tell him as the door swings shut.

Caroline calls over after dark. I'm expecting her. In fact I've rustled up a culinary masterpiece.

'Did Mike ring?' she asks. No smile, nothing. She hovers in the doorway.

I tell her to sit. 'I made your favourite.' I've also opened a bottle of claret, perfect with steak. Caroline appreciates good cuisine, and I'm a fairly decent cook: steaks, stir-fries, Sunday roasts, that sort of thing.

She fiddles with her watch – the one I bought her for her last birthday, a genuine crocodile strap – and tells me she's not hungry.

'You will be.'

I finish laying the table. There are no candles to hand, so I light the kerosene lamp and switch off the main light. I move the dirty cups off the work surface and dump them in the sink. Since Monica stopped cleaning, the place has started smelling a bit. When I turn off the grill, Caroline is standing with her fist around the door knob.

'Come on. Just sit.' I pour the wine. I need her to stay, at least for a while. Truth is, I'm bloody lonely without her.

The wine licks the sides of the glasses before it settles. I take a sip.

'Why are you doing this?' she asks, so quietly I can barely hear. 'Why aren't you out there with us? Don't you care?'

'Of course I do.' I've been trying to hold this town together, get a fence put up, reassure people. That's my job. I can't give up like the rest of them.

'Eddie.' She stares at me. 'What's going on?'

I pull out a chair for her. She hesitates before stepping forward. Her hair is all over the place, she has no make-up on, and is still in the same pale blue dress she wore yesterday and the day before; this is a woman who prides herself on her appearance. And yet she looks more beautiful than ever. I stand behind her until she finally sits.

'Eat this and then we'll go. I'll drive us out along the Wattle Creek road. We can use the spotlight.'

I dish up the food and sit at the other side of the table. 'She could turn up ... anywhere.'

Caroline pushes her plate to one side. 'What else haven't you told us?'

I take another sip of wine. 'If I'd have known ... I didn't think it mattered.'

She jumps up, jerking the table, spilling wine. 'Two people disappear and you don't think it matters? My God, Eddie, you're a heartless bastard. And there was me thinking you might actually feel something.'

'That's not what I meant. I didn't want to scare you, not before we'd found her. Listen to me.' I try to reach her but she pulls away. 'I love you.'

When she turns back, her face has set into a pyramid of dark lines. 'Twenty-three women spent today searching for Georgie, and yesterday, and the day before, and the day before that. We've been searching for two weeks.'

'The police *will* find her.'

'Two detectives with dogs? They're out twelve hours a day. How long do you think it's going to take?'

'They know what they're doing. Come on, eat before it gets cold and then we'll go.' She hasn't eaten properly in days, or slept more than a few hours at a time. You can't expect to think straight like that.

She sits again, out of exhaustion by the looks of it, and watches me eat. I cut a chunk of steak and offer it to her on my fork, but she refuses. In the kerosene light, her face glows. I do really love this woman.

'Have some wine.' I push the glass towards her. 'Where are you going?'

'Out.'

'You'll need some warmer clothes. I'll get you some. Wait here. Why don't you take a shower? You'll feel better. I'll get you something to wear and then we'll go.'

She stops at the door, turning to face me. 'This is *your* favourite, not mine,' she says, gesturing towards the plate.

'Wait,' I say.

I think about the tiny blue vein pulsing in Caroline's neck as I rush out through the shop.

It's cool outside. A constant drone of cicadas shivers through the air. There is a stark quarter moon. The wine has made me feel weightless; my feet skate along. When I pass the truck, I get an idea. I open the shed, pull out the gear and load up the boot, just in case.

The caravan seems to shrink as I approach. Someone has left the door open. I flick on the light and sort through a pile of clothes for some jeans and a long-sleeved blouse. I pick out a few blouses for Caroline to choose from. They smell of her. For a while I forget what I'm doing, even think of lying down and closing my eyes, and then I catch sight of Georgie's clogs. I abandon the clothes on the bed and bend down to pick one up. It's so small, it fits in the palm of my hand, engine red, black laces, like a doll's shoe. My strawberry girl.

I drop the clog, scoop up the clothes, and head out with the smallness of that clog inside me. When I'm halfway across the tarmac, the darkness seems to close in on me. I can't see. I start to run head first. I keep running until I reach the shop. Only when I open the door do I realise how terrified I am.

Caroline is standing by the window in a towel. Her hair is wet. She looks annoyed. 'What took you so long?'

I hand over the clothes and sit on the settee. My cine-camera is out of its case. Monica must have been playing with it. I check the controls and wind it back. She has recorded the model, her hand moving buildings around. I press Record to scrub it out.

'Why did you bring so many clothes?' Caroline asks. That's when I point the camera at her. She has already put on her jeans, and stretches up her arms to slip into her camisole. Her breasts sing white against the t-shirt tan around her neck as the camisole slides over her head. She scowls at me. I keep the camera rolling.

'What are you doing?' she says, slowly buttoning up a white blouse that has faint blue lines running through it, until the lace on her camisole disappears. I stop recording. She moves over to me, takes the camera out of my hands and dumps it roughly on the settee. 'Let's go,' she snaps.

And so we do.

We drive through Akarula Street, past the moon-lit ghost gum. No sign of Mr M. I don't think I've ever seen him after dark. There are no lights on in the houses – as if they are already abandoned. The bar is lit up, and one of the portacabins, probably the detectives' quarters. It makes me wish I'd offered more.

The bush spreads out on either side as we leave the street behind. Caroline leans her head against the window pane.

'Are you still mad with me?' I ask. Her watery expression is hard to read in this patchy light.

We drive for a while in silence. When we are two or three miles away from the town, I pull over, go round the back of the truck, and pop the boot. The rifle is loaded. I take out two pairs of gloves to stop our hands from slipping.

'Put these on,' I tell her, passing her a pair through the window.

'What for? What are you doing with that gun?'

'You drive. Put the gloves on.'

She refuses the gloves but clambers over to the driver's seat and starts the ignition. I slide in beside her and hook my arm out of the open window, positioning the rifle so that it points straight ahead.

'What's going on? You're scaring me.' Her arms are shaking.

'Put the headlights on full.' The adrenalin pumps through me, hardening my muscles, making the underside of my skin feel electrified. Did you ever feel that rush, where your whole body is exploding? Like the second before you peak. It's the best way to let go, to forget. I stick my head out of the window. The wind batters my face.

'Faster,' I shout, banging on the side of the door as if I'm whipping a racehorse.

'Are you trying to get us killed?'

I spot the first kangaroo, bounding out from the right. I let it get to the edge of the road before I fire. Caroline slams on the brakes. I almost drop the rifle as I lunge forward, hanging onto the windscreen from both sides.

'What the hell are you doing?' she screams.

I hand her the rifle and leap out of the truck to get a look. A big red. Still breathing.

'Need to finish him off,' I say, turning back for the rifle.

Caroline gets out of the truck and walks past me. 'Stand back,' she says, and then she fires three bullets. The animal flinches once and slackens with the last breath. When she looks at me, her eyes have emptied out. 'Now *you*. I'll give you five minutes to make a run for it.'

I laugh and walk towards her, but she flips the safety catch off and tenses her finger against the trigger.

'Come on, Caroline. It's not a toy.'

'No? Then what kind of game is this? You said we were coming out to look for Georgie. What the hell were you thinking?'

'I thought you might enjoy it – take your mind off things.'

'You thought I might enjoy killing kangaroos? Are you out of your mind?'

'They're only animals.'

'We're only animals, as you've just illustrated so brilliantly.'

I need to take a leak, so I slowly turn away and unzip my trousers. It's a while before I manage; not that easy when someone is pointing a gun at your back. When I'm finished, her fury seems to have subsided.

'Since when have you liked killing kangaroos?' she asks.

'I used to shoot with some of the fellas from town a couple of years ago. We stopped after Ted went missing. Can you point that somewhere else?' She fastens the safety catch and rests the rifle on the ground. 'Where did you learn to shoot?'

'Dad taught me.' Twisting the barrel in the dirt, she says, 'I used to practise on magpies.'

'I'm sorry, Caroline. I … well, there has to be some way of escaping all this. I know how hard the last two weeks has been for you, and I just thought…I want you to be happy.'

'You want me to be happy? You go blundering on with every half-notion you get in that stupid head of yours, without the slightest idea of what the consequences might be. You'll eat this. I'll make sure you eat every last scrap, because otherwise it was killed for nothing. You can't go killing something for nothing. Do you understand? Everything comes with a price. You can't carry on as if the real world doesn't exist.' She points the gun at the kangaroo and says 'This is the real world, Eddie.'

Her eyes shine out of the dark moon wall behind her.

'You're amazing,' I say, because in that moment she is everything. She somehow fills the whole sky. 'Mike has no idea how amazing you are.'

She looks at me for a second and then her gaze drifts over my shoulder. 'I'm a bad mother and a worse wife. Maybe – if I hadn't met Michael, if I hadn't got pregnant – I would have been a mediocre singer. I was doing alright. But that's not who I am. I'm sick of being something you dreamed up. I just want Georgie back.'

She carries on, but her words melt away until all I can hear is the rhythm of her voice. I clutch her around the waist, lift her off the ground and spin her around and around. I keep spinning, she keeps shouting as she pounds my head and shoulders. For a moment, we're inseparable.

I lose the tread of my feet and cling on to her to steady myself, ignoring the whirring thud in my head. Eventually she breaks free of me and dives off into the bush. She starts yelling out *Georgie*. If you could hear her now: like a whale, like she is calling from the deep. That's when I know for certain that we will never find Georgie or the others. They are gone, lost, irretrievable.

I chase Caroline in and out of the moonlight. When I catch her up, we call out George's name together for a while before I manage to draw her back. We have no torch, only the spotlight on the truck.

On the road, we crouch down beside the carcass.

'This has to be the worst idea you've ever had,' she says, hugging her knees up to her chest. 'Promise me you'll never get an idea like this again.'

'I promise.'

'You'd promise anything, wouldn't you? Do you remember what you said? A small paradise. That our lives would be transformed. They've been transformed alright. Is this your idea of paradise?'

'I thought you'd thank me for taking you away from all that.'

'*All that* was my life, Eddie. *All that* was my daughters and my husband.' She stares at me. 'You know as well as I do that Georgie's probably dead by now.' When she realises what she has said, she stops breathing. I take her shoulders and shake her until she cries, long pitiful cries. We hold hands as if we're both clinging onto a safety rope, but I can't feel her. I can't feel anything.

'Tell me what to do,' I say. 'I don't know what to do.'

She pulls her hand out of mine, wiping the tears from her face, and then she takes hold of the hind legs of the kangaroo, signalling for me to lift its torso. We drag the thing across the dirt, hoisting it up onto the back seat. It weighs a ton. With the seats pushed forward, we just about fit it in.

Caroline drives back with the radio on, a reporter talking about the Queen's visit next month and what will be spent on security. The presenter plays 'The White Cliffs of Dover' and some sixties' tune. By the time we pull into the service station, I am miles away.

When the engine stops, I turn around to look at the dead roo lying on the back seat, and wonder if it would be so bad, having all the lights turned out.

As Caroline unfastens her seat belt, she looks at me, her eyes magnified by the dark circles around them. 'Would it have made any difference if you'd known?'

'Known what?'

She draws her lips in before she says, 'Georgie is your daughter.'

I look up at the roof and see thousands of tiny holes in the brown material. I keep looking at the holes as the truck door opens and she gets out.

'I guess not,' she says, slamming the door.

So many holes. You'd never count them all.

CAROLINE

Last night I pictured Georgie on a white beach. She was crawling towards the sea. The beach went on for ever, and the tide kept going out. I was hovering above her like one of those awful birds of prey. I tried to swoop down, but I couldn't. It was impossible to reach her.

I'm smoking on the caravan steps when Michael's plane arrives from Wattle Creek. The thought of seeing him and Moni gives me a dull ache in my chest, although I still feel numb. And lonely as hell. I was always afraid of being alone. As a child, I used to stand in front of the sea on one of those slate grey English days and wait for it to swallow me. It almost did, once.

I grew up by the sea. Whitley Bay. My parents ran a guest house. Well, my mother ran the guest house. Dad spent most of his time pipe-smoking on the porch and shooting magpies. Good old Mum trailed around after him like one of those tin cans that gets tied to the back of a wedding car. I suppose none of us know what kind of ride we're in for when we say our marriage vows and make those hefty promises. Mum and I tried so hard to please that man. He loved Moni, treated her like a queen – I could never understand that. Poor Georgie missed out altogether. We stopped visiting. I didn't want him interfering any more, judging Georgie, favouring Moni, making us all feel inadequate. *You should have been watching her; it's more than careless for a mother to lose her child.* His voice inside my head is so loud, it nearly deafens me.

If I concentrate, I can make myself stop thinking for seconds at a time. When my mind empties out, I feel alright. Until I remember.

A cloud of red dust, turbulence from the plane, blows over the tarmac and covers the pumps, Eddie's truck, and the back windows of the caravan. There is so much dust. Earlier on I saw three houses being towed away. The removal lorries or road trains or whatever they were, pulled in to fill up with petrol, a house on the back of each. I don't know whose houses they were – the houses in the street are all identical. I asked one of the drivers where he was taking them.

'Adelaide,' he said. 'It's a good fifteen-hour drive from here.' The way he scratched the stubble on his chin made me think he knew something about Georgie, that there was some kind of hidden conspiracy. I've been thinking that a lot lately. 'Repossession orders. Some fella named Harvey. What's a woman like you hiding in the bush for?' He was a big man: big chest, big legs, crude pushy eyes.

'First time I've seen a house moved,' I said, conscious of my English accent, which made me feel strangely vulnerable.

'These houses are built to be trucked around. People get attached. They want to move, they move the house. Makes sense to me.' He winked before strolling off to talk to one of the other drivers.

I've got used to the Australian men. They have a different approach to women than in England, something more basic, more real perhaps. (I'm not a feminist like my daughter. Moni didn't get that from me. Mostly she takes after her dad.)

Michael appears on the road, carrying Moni, with the overnight bag slung on his back like a rucksack. He looks young from this distance, carefree, the way he walks as if Moni weighs nothing at all. I call over, flinging what's left of my cigarette on the ground before running towards them. I imagine wrapping my arms around their necks, Georgie standing in the middle of us, her little hands tight over her head like a crash helmet, guarding against our affections. And it hurts; it hurts so much I can't even cry.

Moni is barely awake. She brushes her wrist over my ear. I want to hold her, but she clings to her dad. Besides, she's too heavy for me. Michael doesn't say a word, so I race ahead into the shop, talking rubbish. I'm afraid of what he's going to tell me.

'What did they say? Did you see Susan? You must be hungry. We've got eggs. I'll make some eggs.'

Michael stops in the doorway. His whole body slumps as he lowers Moni to the floor. The distance in his bloodshot eyes makes my heart sink. We go through to the sitting room, the three of us, and Michael helps Moni onto the camp bed. Within seconds she's asleep.

'Is she alright?' I whisper, perching on the arm of the settee.

'Seems she was lucky.'

'What did they say … about her talking like Georgie?'

'Shock. We need to keep her busy. Susan said it's just a matter of time until she comes to terms with what's happened.'

I nod, looking past him through the window at the cloudless sky. That dull ache in my chest throbs again. 'What has happened?' I blurt out.

My husband gapes at me while he tries to organise his words. Eventually he says, 'She's got to take two of these every night. They'll help her sleep,' plucking a box of pills from the overnight bag. 'Where's Eddie?'

'Must have got an early start. We went for a drive last night, to see if… He shot a kangaroo.' I don't know why I tell Michael this, except that I want him to know *everything*. Finally. I want it all to be over.

Michael looks right through me. His breath is paper thin; I can almost see it. I swat a fly off my sandal and then move Eddie's cine-camera out of the way so that he can sit. He stretches his legs underneath the table, and I reach out and stroke his forehead. It feels odd, touching him this way after so long. When he looks up at me, I draw back, only my hand stays stretched out for a moment as if it doesn't know what to do. He says: 'We're going to get through this, whatever happens. We're going to pray for a miracle.' Then he reaches over and takes my hand, pressing it to his cheek before kissing my palm, softly tracing my life-line with his fingertip. If he knew what I have done....

'Eggs,' I say, pulling away.

He stands. 'I'm going out. Will you watch Moni?' But he doesn't go.

Moni is snoring, little snuffling grunts like puffs of smoke. We listen together for a second, sharing one of those moments that define us as parents, that makes us the Harvey Family. And then I rush through to the kitchen and throw on some eggs and toast, losing myself in the shine of the metal ladle, the click of the toaster, the small pool of water collected on the draining board. Maybe Michael is right: we will find our little girl. *Pray for a miracle.* My hands lay the table as if they are doing it without me, placing each plate symmetrically on the chequered cloth so that the setting has a clear order and the stains are covered up. The threads of sunlight pushing through the filthy window make the plates glint religiously. Underneath my breath I say a prayer, the same prayer, over and over, while slipping off my flip flops – cool tiles against the soles of my feet – and I am empty.

Hearing the sitting-room door close, I shout: 'Take this with you,' forgetting that Moni is asleep. I quickly stack some toast into a lunch box and go through to the hall, calling again until I see him at the other end. He is holding Eddie's cine-camera. I can't read his face properly in the gritty wall-light, but his hands are shaking, and when I get close, I see sweat or tears falling onto the camera. 'Michael?' It is a few seconds before I remember, before I see what he has just seen in rapid flashes that pass so quickly they barely have time to form. I have nothing to say. *How could you lose your own daughter? What were you doing?* That. I was doing that. Eventually I whisper: 'What's wrong?' as if I didn't know. He drops the camera on the hall floor, waking Moni, and with a glazed expression on his wet face, walks through to the shop. Something indescribable breaks between us.

I've been waiting for this moment, picturing Michael's fury in my head. But this silence is worse than anything either of us might have said. Michael has always hated conflict. Every argument we've ever had ends up with him taking refuge in a newspaper, or walking out, while I carry on shouting. But in a strange way, now that it's done, I feel lighter, anaesthetised. *You had it coming. Serves you right. Don't come crying to me.*

The tape is still running when I pick up the cine-camera, just a blank screen. I go into the sitting room and throw the vile thing onto the settee, along with the lunch box.

Moni is bent forwards, holding onto her knees, gibbering at the wall in front of her. 'Did you see them? Who locked them behind those doors? Georgie can't get out.'

When I go over, her voice gets more panicked. I kneel beside the camp bed and take hold of her arms. 'You were dreaming. It's just a dream. Come on, let's blow it away.' I blow, letting go of her arms, and tinkle my fingers in the air as if I can see the dream fritter into nothing. But Moni can't see it; she can't see anything. She is no longer four years old, when these things used to work magic. Where did the time go?

I can feel her shrinking away from me. The loneliness of the last two weeks sits between us like a judge – she doesn't seem to recognise my face.

'Moni, please,' I beg. She turns to the wall.

She has grown thin, withered, like a victim of war. Everything has changed. Even this room looks starker, or else I hadn't noticed the lack of paintings before. And it scares me. It terrifies me, being this close to the edge.

Eddie doesn't come back until mid-afternoon, when he collapses in a chair and closes his eyes.

'What is it?' I ask, laying down the book I've been reading to Moni. He knows something; he has found something. I stand up, feeling my body go hard so that whatever he throws at me won't get through. 'Eddie?' He doesn't answer me, keeps his eyes shut. 'Eddie!' I go over to him, reach out and grab his arms tightly as I shout into his self-affirming ears: 'Where have you been?'

His eyes flash open, and for a second he stares at Moni – she has picked up the book and seems engrossed – then he clutches the seat cushion on either side of his legs, straightening up, and starts in a whisper. 'I thought I'd find her. I woke up knowing where she was. I ran as fast as I could to the mine track. She was lying on the ground. I saw her, I almost saw her there.' He stops, defeated. When he eventually carries on, his voice has levelled out into a flat bass note. 'I was so sure she was there.' He lets out this pitiable cry that frightens Moni.

I help her out of the bed and coax her into the hall. 'Wait here.'

Then I go back to Eddie. 'Did you see Michael? Did you talk to him?' He shakes his head. I don't tell him that Michael knows. It hardly seems to matter. 'Are you trying to say that after all this time you've decided to look for Georgie? Is that it?'

'I looked everywhere.'

The storm inside me finally breaks, and it is over, wiped out, as if we never really began. When I leave, I feel as if I'm closing the door on a stranger.

Karlin is serving the red-necked woman who lives opposite Maddie. She lifts up the counter flap and pushes out a stool for me to sit on. 'You alright, honey? Can I get you anything?'

I bundle Moni onto the stool. The other woman – it is not just her neck, her whole face is red-swollen with a grainy finish – pushes her petrol coupons across the counter. She says: 'I'll be going out again this afternoon,' obviously feeling that she needs to excuse herself for doing something else.

'I appreciate your help,' I say. And I do, I really do; they've all been so good. The red-necked woman presses my arm before she leaves. Though I smile, I could scream at her. None of them have any idea what it is like: being plagued by the fear of what Georgie might be going through, and not being able to help. There could not be a worse form of torture. I sometimes think it would be easier if we knew Georgie were dead.

When the door closes behind her, I ask Karlin to mind Moni for an hour or two. 'Maddie said she'd help me look around the mine road again.'

Her breath stops just short of a sigh. 'You do what you have to do,' she says, scooping the money and coupons off the counter and slipping them into the register. 'Of course I'll watch her.' She swings round to Moni. 'We've got plenty of pricing to do.' Then she runs her hand up along the length of her other arm from her wrist to her elbow, as if she's pushing back a sleeve, before grabbing a handful of mint mojos from the jar beside the till. She tips them into Moni's hands.

'What do you say?' I prompt, hating myself for sounding like my dad.

'Thank you,' Moni says in a perfunctory way, adding, 'These are Georgie's favourite.' She is right; they are Georgie's favourite, those and the strawberry ones. Karlin nods, attempting to hold a neutral face, but the corners of her mouth twitch a little.

I wave back at Moni, who is peeling the wrapper from a sweet, and wonder how we ever reached this point.

Maddie meets me on the road. With her plaid shirt tucked into the waistband of her trousers, she looks like a man.

'I was just on my way,' she says, tugging her cotton head scarf further forward to shield her eyes. 'Saw Michael this morning. He needs to take a break. He was staggering. You don't look much better yourself. I suppose you've heard the latest?' I wait for her to carry on. 'There's a fence being put up, a great big bastard of a thing. The gates are already rigged across the road.' We walk together as Maddie points over to the men in the distance working on the fence. It looks hideous.

'Do you know where Michael is?' I ask.

'Heading to the mine with those detectives.' She doesn't say it, but I know she's thinking what they are all thinking – that we've looked everywhere.

We walk towards Mr M, who is sheltering underneath the tree. It's a beautiful tree, maybe more so because it's the only one. With its white bark, and the way the branches twist out like arms, it seems almost human.

'Look at him,' Maddie says scornfully. 'You'd think he'd be ashamed to sit around while the rest of us are searching night and day. God knows we've raked every inch.' Maddie sucks in her lips for a second before starting to say something else, but then she stops halfway through a sentence. Once we get level with Mr M, I turn and head straight over to the tree without

91

knowing quite why. I've never spoken to him before. We've exchanged smiles and waves when I've picked up the girls, but we've never actually spoken. Yet I feel as if he knows me. Moni used to sit with him for hours. Of course now she's not allowed out on her own.

I try to speak but nothing comes and so I stand there in a haze of silence.

He remains motionless, a quiet silvery expression playing across his face, and then he says: 'I'm sorry your daughter's gone. I don't know why it had to be a child.' He doesn't look at me but at my shadow, running his eyes along the outline.

I gaze at him for a while, speechless.

Maddie's voice makes me flinch. 'Caroline!'

And still I can't find a way to leave. Georgie thought the world of him. She and Moni drew his portrait. I've got them stuck up on the caravan wall: squiggles really, in Georgie's case anyway, but somehow she managed to capture him. As he slowly lifts his eyes to look at me, I feel as if I know what he is thinking, almost, as if he is telling me whatever it is I need to know. I don't move until I feel Maddie's hand on my arm. She yanks me away forcefully.

When we get back to the road, she starts. 'You're better off leaving him alone. Let the police sort it out.'

'Sort what out?'

'Let them do their job.'

I haven't got the heart to continue this discussion.

We walk right through the street and out the other side, picking up ten or so women on the way. I can't get Mr M out of my mind. He has one of those oak-aged faces that are timeless: full of trees and rivers and wild animals. He blends into the landscape as if he belongs, as if he was born from that tree. Georgie used to call him Markarrwala; he even warranted her favourite word, BLAST, a word reserved for the privileged few.

We spread out in a line and study the ground. It's like a ritual we are bound by, these daily searches. When I'm out, raking the ground for clues, I feel released – the simple act of moving frees my mind. Do I believe she's still alive after fifteen days? I don't know. Not really. The odds are close to impossible, but there is always that tiny whisper of hope. Without that, I couldn't go on.

After an hour or so, my neck starts to ache and the ridges and small mounds that jut out just above the surface seem huge and insurmountable. I forget I am surrounded by endless space. We don't talk much; there is nothing to say. Every now and then someone finds a drinks bottle, a pen or a coin, and we all take a look to see if it can tell us more than the fact that someone dropped it there. Every time something is found, I feel myself break away from my skin. The objects are put into a plastic bag, just in case, and passed on to the detectives.

We find a crisp packet that has been shrunk in a fire, what looks like the needle from a watch, and a ring, a copper ring. I try to inject them all with meaning, but it's hard, after all this time. I am so tired.

In a few hours we head back, past the stretch of fence that snakes around the street and part of the old mine, penning us in like cattle. Against the fading light, the wire looks ominous. Maddie suggests a drink.

'I'm going to check on Moni,' I say, thanking the women individually.

But Maddie insists. 'You'll be no use to anyone if you don't mind yourself.'

The rest of the women hustle me into the bar before I get a chance to object.

A few men playing pool look up as we take our seats. They don't know what to say. No one really knows what to say anymore. The two detectives are sitting at the counter having supper. When Delaney spots me, she comes over, pulling up a stool next to mine. She doesn't need to explain that they have found nothing more. It's written all over her face.

'We'll be leaving tomorrow,' she says, prodding a finger in her teeth, fishing out the remnants of whatever she has just eaten. 'Your daughter may have been taken away, either by road or air. We've alerted police stations across the country. They've all got a photograph of Georgina. There's nothing more we can do, I'm afraid.' She locks her hands together in a patronising way. 'If she's been taken away, we have a chance of finding her. Your husband gave me a recent photograph.'

'Where is he?'

She shrugs; it seems an effort for her to lift her bulky shoulders.

I'm glad to escape. Dusk reddens the sky as I walk through the street towards the service station, past what would have been the last house, now a naked patch of land with a poorly kept lawn in front. I stop at the edge of the bush, where the road bends round, at the point where you can no longer see the street. With what is left of me, I make my plea: *Please come back. I should have told you every day how much I loved you. We'll keep looking. We'll look for as long as it takes. Pleeease come back.* I can't tell whether the words leave my mouth or not. My legs give way and I slump down in the dirt. I keep talking to Georgie, trying to see her in my mind's eye, but everything is blurred.

Michael's voice echoes in my ear and then I feel him wrap his arm around my waist and pull me up. Even now, I can't tell if I am dreaming.

'Come on,' he says, gently easing me forwards as I lean into him. We follow the beam of the torch, staying in the centre of the road to avoid the ruts that have been driven deep by removal trucks. I want to beg him to forgive me, but I can't seem to find a single word, and so I let him talk.

'Karlin went home. Eddie's looking after Moni. He was out all day. Says as soon as I get back, he'll go out again.' There is no trace of anger or sadness in his voice, just quiet resignation. 'You need to sleep.'

My mouth is so dry it hurts. He leads me through the open area of the service station towards the caravan and helps me up the steps.

'Aren't you going to say something?' I ask, willing him to shout at me.

'There's some pasta in the pan.' He turns away. 'I made it about an hour ago. I'll sleep with Moni tonight.'

'Will you stay for a minute?'

His boots echo against the tarmac as he leaves.

I lie on our bed, fully clothed, and gaze up at the peeling yellow paintwork on the ceiling. There is a crack running right down the wall. Michael didn't want to move here; he came because of me. I convinced him, making out this place was a palace, our very own holiday home. It was me who stuck those stupid pictures on the wall. I bought them in Wattle Creek: Sydney Harbour, Ayres Rock, a dazed-looking koala bear. Who was I kidding? I thought if we were somewhere new, things might go back to normal, to how they were before Michael drove into that boy. I thought we could build the kind of life we always wanted for the girls. I actually believed it was possible to live that dream Eddie had spun so perfectly. Eddie doesn't care about me, not really. What he cares about is his precious town. But these people aren't cardboard cut-outs he can just move around and buy off every once in a while. They'll move. We'd still be in England if I hadn't insisted, getting on with our small lives that weren't that bad. All four of us.

A few weeks ago, Michael was talking about going home. I told him we should stay another month. Eddie had promised us a house; I wanted so much for us to have our own house. Or was it that I wanted Eddie? Why didn't I listen? I knew he was right.

While we wait for Maddie, I pace in front of the sitting-room window, going over the words of a new song in my head. I revise the longer lines, knocking out surplus notes, and then I try singing the whole thing out loud. Moni stops writing in her notebook and listens intently. Because I can't get through the whole verse, I end up whispering the last line.

Moni says, 'Georgie will like that.'

'Do you like it?'

'Not much.'

'Why not?'

'It made you cry.'

I look out at the caravan for a while, and then say, 'Why don't we make your dad some lunch.'

'It's not lunchtime.'

'It will be.'

Moni grudgingly follows me into the kitchen. I cut the bread and do the pasting while she wraps. We make a few extra rounds for the women.

As I'm packing the sandwiches into a bag, Moni asks, 'Do dead babies float?'

I have no reply, so she goes on.

'If their stomachs blow up like balloons, they'll float. I was wondering....'

'Pass me that knife.' How does she get such thoughts in her head?

Thankfully Maddie arrives, but the damage is done. Now I have this image of babies floating down a river, hundreds of them, bobbing around like plastic dolls.

'What are you up to?' Maddie asks, her broad face creased in a thin smile. 'By the way, I just saw the Wartons leaving. I think Queeny's taking over the store until the place clears out. Her hubby's decided to jack in the mine and help too. They've said they'll stay to the end.' Though she is still smiling, the lines on her forehead deepen.

'There's plenty of beer in the cool box. Help yourself,' I say.

'Don't be out there all day.' She taps my arm.

'Thanks for this.'

I check around, feeling as if I've forgotten something. 'I won't be long,' I tell Moni as I leave. She ignores me, too busy drawing some poor insect she has imprisoned in that matchbox of hers.

Michael is standing on the tarmac, squinting up at three parrots perched on the roof. His legs have regained their muscular appearance; he looks fitter with his brown skin.

'I forgot my sunglasses,' he says when he sees me.

I stand close to him and watch the birds gather air under their wings to cool off. 'I made you sandwiches.'

'No thanks.'

(We're all sick and tired of sandwiches.)

'They look sad,' I say. The largeness of the sky seems to shrink the parrots into mantelpiece ornaments. 'Can I come with you?'

'If you want. Eddie is on the other side of the mine.'

Michael suddenly takes off. I try to keep up. We don't talk, just scan the road for signs. A sense of hopelessness takes over me; the farther we go, the worse it gets. When we reach the scrub grass on the other side of the street, Michael says: 'I'd prefer to do this on my own.'

I nod and start walking away from him; it is as though we are already miles apart. After some time, the sandwiches weigh heavy, so I take them out of their wrapping and break them up, letting the crumbs fall to the ground.

Moni makes me wear the plain green thin-strapped dress with the patent cream belt and cream piped edging.

'It's Dad's favourite,' she says. 'He'll be disappointed if you don't dress up.'

(I always dress up for Michael's birthday.) She pulls out the pair of pearl earrings Michael bought me for our fifth wedding anniversary, and insists I paint my lips and spray perfume on my wrists.

'That's disgusting,' she says, flaring her nostrils at the smell.

I switch off the oven and lift out the cake. Perhaps she's right. We can't go on ignoring life.

'Have you got Dad's present?' I ask. The David Attenborough book we ordered came in on the mail plane last week.

After a slapdash icing session, Moni mounts the cake on a plate and carries it outside. It seems to take us for ever to reach the house, with Moni doing pigeon steps so as not to upset the cake. As we pass through the shop, Karlin tells us that Eddie has been out since daybreak. Thank God. I can't bear the idea of seeing him.

'Dad!' Moni shouts from the sitting room.

Michael comes out of the office. On seeing me all dressed up, his face tightens with confusion. I feel ashamed. It's wrong to do this when Georgie is… but for Moni's sake, I carry on.

'What's this?' he asks, staying where he is.

'Nothing,' Moni says, grinning at him as she hides the cake behind the settee and then bobs down to light the candles.

We sing Happy Birthday. It feels like the saddest song in the world. But then he smiles at Moni and acts the clown, dancing around her like he always does on *her* birthday. Keeping my promise to Moni, I dust off the record player and flip through Eddie's albums, choosing Elvis Presley, one of Michael's favourites. He used to do a great Elvis impression.

While he cuts the cake, I set the needle on the record. The first track is 'Blue Suede Shoes'. Moni takes Michael's hand and gets him dancing. She reaches out for my hand too, and all three of us dance in a sort of wavy line around the room, joining in with the song.

When the next track begins, Moni stops dancing and asks: 'Where is it?'

'Where's what?' I am afraid she's going to start raving on again about Georgie being locked away, but instead she peers around the back of the settee and underneath the table.

'Dad's present,' she says.

'By the record player.'

'Not that one. The present from Uncle Eddie.'

'You'll have to ask him. Here you go.' I hand her the book to give to Michael, which she thrusts at him impatiently.

He makes the usual fuss and the pair of them sits together on the settee, flicking through the photographs. I continue to dance on my own, even though the music has stopped.

The next day Eddie bursts into the caravan, jabbering something about the mine closing down. He hangs onto the doorframe as he speaks. 'It's not legal. We have to stop them. Where's Michael? Let's go.' He's hyperventilating from running in the heat and can barely see for the sweat clouding his eyes.

'I have to stay with Moni.'

'Come on, Monica, we need your help.' He claps his hands at her.

She is absorbed in a new book she has found, but eventually she looks up, nodding at her uncle as she slides her feet into her flip flops.

I wrap a scarf around my head. 'What's the rush? I ask. 'If they're closing the mine, there's not a lot we can do about it.'

'Not enough miners they say. That's bullshit.' He shepherds Moni out as he continues. 'They've been against me from the start. If John was still alive, he'd have sorted this out. I should have seen it coming.'

I've no idea what he is talking about. His obsession with this town would be almost comical if it weren't so grotesque. But I follow him across the tarmac anyway; we both do. He has developed a stoop from constantly tilting his head towards the ground. Michael has somehow grown taller and Eddie looks like a stunted old man.

Moni drops back and yanks my arm. 'When are we leaving?' Michael's been filling her head with the idea of moving to Adelaide. He thinks we should carry on looking for Georgie there, but we won't find her in Adelaide. She didn't disappear in Adelaide. He says it will be better for Moni. Seemingly the doctor, Susan, agrees, although I suspect the whole thing was her idea in the first place.

'We're not going anywhere just yet,' I tell Moni.

'Everyone else is leaving.'

'Well….'

'Georgie isn't here.'

'Shut up.' I don't mean to snap.

Eddie leads us past the service station and on towards the bend in the road, continuing to jabber away to himself. His save-my-town speech would have infuriated me a few days ago, but

I am past caring. He spins around to face us, gesturing at Moni until she speeds up to walk beside him.

'Why did those men put up that fence?' she asks.

'To keep us safe.'

I elaborate on Eddie's weak explanation. 'It's your Uncle Eddie's idea of a joke.'

Moni narrows her eyes, looking utterly confused.

We continue walking in a line. Just before we reach the bend, Eddie says: 'They don't feel safe. Nobody gets a good night's sleep. I see my houses being driven off and I can't stop them. There'll be no one left.'

'Stop it,' I tell him.

Seconds later, Moni shouts, pointing frantically at a small group of people who are watching one of the houses being craned onto a removal truck.

'I thought they were your houses, Uncle Eddie?' she says.

'They are.' Eddie breaks into a run.

I search the faces, looking for Michael, but he's not there. Maddie calls me over, waving a piece of paper in the air. When we reach her, she thrusts the paper towards me.

'We've been given our marching orders,' she says.

I scan the notice, and look up to see Eddie barging his way through the spectators towards the crane.

Maddie goes on to explain, 'The bank is taking the rest of the houses within the week. Someone's not been paying the bills.' Her voice dissolves into the wash of noise.

I watch Eddie on the other side of the road. His face pales as another of the houses gets winched up onto the back of an articulated lorry. He darts over to the lorry, shouting, and tries to pull the driver out. There is so much noise and dust. And suddenly Eddie is lying right in front of the lorry in the middle of the road. I feel myself drifting off, up and away, as Mr M emerges from the crowd and crouches down beside Eddie. I see all this from a height. Someone throws a stone; it catches the side of Eddie's head. Mr M takes Eddie by his arms and drags him to the side of the road. That's when I come crashing back down.

The morning heat is thickening. I flick on the fan. My legs are aching and there's a blister on my neck where I forgot the sun cream. My reflection in the dark-veined mirror on the back of the wardrobe door startles me. I am all bone. No one can tell you what it's like to lose a child. Wherever you go, whatever you do, the sense of loss clings to you like a rotten corpse. But it's not like that either. It's not like anything.

They are calling today the final search. Surely the final search is the one where we find her? You don't stop looking because someone decided eighteen days was the deadline. There are no deadlines when people disappear. I mark the calendar nailed onto the back of the caravan door with another diagonal strike of blue ink. As I step back, the strikes seem to topple like a stack of dominoes.

I lift the net curtains above the sink and tuck them over the plastic-coated wire. Michael is standing by the pumps talking to Jake, whose large mouth sags a little as he points out something on the map they are holding between them. The map sags too. They must be planning the search. I've agreed to stay with Moni. All the women – there aren't many – are sitting this one out: packing up, getting ready to move apparently. What do they imagine will happen if we don't find her? That the book will be closed? A line will be drawn under this whole unfortunate incident – which is how I've heard people talk about Georgie's disappearance. I don't blame them. I would have left at the first sign of trouble had Georgie been someone else's child. But they can't leave; we're all jailed in by this ridiculous fence.

Michael glances up from the map and sees me – at least I think he does – but then he looks back down, shielding the side of his face with one hand against the sun. Jake Brenton gets into his blue station wagon and drives off. And I watch the man I fell in love with sixteen years ago walk around the petrol pumps and disappear behind the front wall of the service station.

We don't sleep together. Michael hasn't touched me since the day he saw the cine-camera, not that he touched me much before, not since his depression, but I always felt he cared. I always knew he loved me. Not now. I grab a dirty t-shirt and rub a clean spot in the window, which hasn't been wiped in weeks. One day of dust is enough to block the view. Maybe Michael couldn't see me for the dust?

I should feed the birds. Three of them, galahs, are waiting patiently on the telegraph wire. Michael has neglected them lately. I don't agree with feeding wild birds, but once you start, you have to carry on.

In an attempt to boil some water, I strike four matches before I manage to light the stove. All the cups are stained. I scour the coronation mug to get rid of the tide-marks; they won't come out. While I'm waiting for the kettle to boil, I rewrap Georgie's clothes: a Wombles t-shirt, her favourite skirt, and the spotted socks she likes. Clean clothes for when … I put the skirt on the cushion first, then the t-shirt, resting her socks on top. It doesn't look right. I have to move the socks to one side – which socks did she have on that day? Then I put the socks back on top again. The kettle whistles, filling the caravan with steam. I switch off the fan, lift the kettle from the boil, and go out to find Moni.

At the pumps, the red-necked woman is filling her battered ute with petrol. When I reach her, she starts telling me that her house will be taken tomorrow. She's got family north of Adelaide. After she has slotted the nozzle back into the pump slot, she wipes her hands down her baggy cotton trousers, still talking. Her lilting voice follows me around the pumps as I head into the service station shop.

There is no one behind the counter. Karlin left days ago. It seems Eddie is trusting people to put their money in the till while he goes out looking for Georgie. Why does he suddenly care? Shouldn't it be about more than a birthright? Is that what this is all about? Or maybe he's just fretting about his town? He's like a child trying to catch the pieces of a toy airplane that has been shot down.

I call through the hall to Moni. 'Don't forget your hat.' When I open the sitting-room door, I find her crouched down beside the table, staring at Eddie's model town. 'Where's Uncle Eddie?' I ask. 'Where's Dad? Who's looking after you?' She looks at me wistfully, and slowly stands. I talk fast to hurry her up. 'Maddie's leaving tomorrow. We should say goodbye.' Moni's eyes are fringed with tears but there is nothing I can do.

I tousle her hair before I take her hand. She kisses my arm as we go through to the hall. The wet patch where her lips have touched my arm makes my skin tingle. In my head I tell her that I love her. I can't say it out loud. As we pass through the shop, Moni steals a Marathon bar from the sweet rack and stashes it in her shorts pocket. I pretend not to notice. I pretend not to notice that she has one arm stretched out beside her, her hand curved slightly as if she is guiding someone, as if she is holding Georgie's hand.

When we hit the road, we push our way through the heat.

'Is Dad with them?' Moni asks, pointing over to a line of men a good way off on the far side of the fence.

'Your dad will never give up.'

If you look beyond the men, you can see the hazy line of the horizon, marking some kind of ending. In the past few days I've pictured Georgie just beyond that line, an inch farther than I can see.

As we walk towards the bend in the road, Moni scrapes at the edges of the bush with a stick, stopping every few yards to lift up a stone or poke at a tuft of scrub grass, no doubt probing for insects. She has settled down a bit. The medication seems to help. At least she's stopped talking like Georgie, or to Georgie, but I can still feel the ghost of my little girl standing between us.

I see Georgie everywhere: in a clump of grass, in the cloud shadows on the ground. I see her waving at me, smiling, puckering up her lips like she did whenever I presented her with green food, and then her face gets distorted in the light and she fades back into the endless bush. Why didn't I give her longer baths? Why didn't I sing to her every night instead of when I felt like it? For a second, I close my eyes and try to hear the sound of her laughing as I poured the water over her head. I can see her, but I can't hear her. I hear the scraping of Moni's stick on the ground, the call of an occasional bird, a faint distant rumble that could be voices or a car; I can even hear my own breathing, but not Georgie. And then I lose sight of her too. All I see is this corrugated road of red earth that runs right into the sky.

The street is empty, except for Mr M, sitting underneath the white tree. I've often wondered whether he has children, what it was like here before the mine, why he stayed. There are things I'd like to ask him, but not now, so I deliberately veer off towards the other side of the road, passing him at a distance. Then I stop and wait for Moni. She is way behind, rooting in between a cluster of rocks. She doesn't seem to understand what's going on. It's as if this is all a game, as if she's still playing hide and seek. Maybe it is a game. Maybe Eddie's right. We spend our lives learning the rules, and every now and then the rules change, but the game is still the same game.

'Hurry up!' I shout to Moni. It's too hot to be hanging around. She puts something in her pocket and then runs, stopping abruptly beside Mr M. After nodding at him, she starts foraging for small stones.

'Moni!'

She is so intent on collecting stones that she doesn't hear me. (Michael is the same; they both go conveniently deaf when they're concentrating.) Moni places the stones in a ring around Mr M. I can't see his face, but his back slackens; I imagine he is smiling. When she has used the last of the stones, she waves at him and kangaroo-jumps towards me with a big grin on her face.

'What did you do that for?' I ask.

'He told me to. Look!' She points up at a wedge-tailed eagle circling above us. 'Do you think it's hungry?'

They're like vultures, hovering around, swooping down on dead animals and picking the bones clean. I grasp a handful of dried earth and pelt it at the bird, though of course it doesn't actually hit it. Nevertheless, the bird glides off.

'You could have hurt it,' Moni says, her face turning scarlet. She gets her temper from me.

'They're vermin.'

Why would Mr M ask her to do that?

A few yards before the first house – there are seven left – Moni crosses the street to get as far away from me as possible. It can hardly be called a street any more. I imagined something grand, something impressive, the way Eddie wrote about his miraculous town. The saddest thing is that he believed every word. I don't understand why he let himself build up so much debt. These people paid rent. Though one thing Eddie's good at is spending money. Like Maddie said, he's a big fish who built himself too small a pond. But I can't imagine him without this town – this street. He doesn't seem to understand that there will be no Akarula without the mine, no mine without miners, and no one is prepared to live in a place where people disappear.

The men look like small question marks in the distance. There is nowhere we haven't looked. Michael is doing this search for me, for us, for what we used to be. He doesn't really believe… I wave Moni over to Maddie's house, which stands between the store and the bar. She crosses the road to join me, scowling. While I wait for her on Maddie's patch of garden – a square of lawn resembling burnt toast – I pick the dirt from my nails.

'Sorry,' I say, when she is a few steps away.

'It's alright.'

I know it'll be at least a day before I'm properly forgiven.

Moni marches past me and knocks on Maddie's door. I don't know how I would have survived this town without Maddie. At the same time, I can't imagine knowing her anywhere else, meeting her in England, for example, or even in Adelaide. We're so different. The only thing that unites us is this town. It's the same with all the women.

Maddie hollers out, 'It's open,' poking her head around the kitchen door as we step inside. She gives me one of her bear hugs. Her breath is rancid from drink. 'I'm up to my neck in boxes. We're meeting in the bar. The women want to say goodbye.' She bends down to whisper in Moni's ear. 'You fancy a Coke?'

Moni softens under Maddie's generous smile. 'Yes please.' She doesn't even like Coke.

'I'm not sure I…'

'Nonsense,' Maddie interrupts, pushing her wiry hair off her face as she looks at me. 'It'll take your mind off things. There's nothing we can do now except wait. Queeny said the detectives flew in. I think they went out with Michael earlier on. Maybe they know something we don't.'

I get a sudden surge of hope; it fills me to the brim. Maddie's right; they must know something we don't.

Dropping her gaze back to Moni, Maddie says, 'How you keeping? Your dad told me you've been up to the hospital again.'

Moni nods before rummaging through her rucksack, producing her notebook and the matchbox. 'Do you want to see it?'

'What you got in there this time?'

'A beetle. Not sure what sort. My dad will know.' She sticks the matchbox underneath Maddie's nose and slides it open.

'My God, that's some smell.'

'They do that when they're scared. It's a defence mechanism.'

'Defence mechanism. Where do you learn phrases like that? You're a walking dictionary.'

'Dad told me.'

'That's enough,' I say, trying to take the matchbox, but she's too quick. 'Put the poor creature outside.'

'Dad hasn't seen it yet.'

It's Michael's fault, this fascination she has with insects. He encourages her.

Maddie chivvies us on. 'We can't sit here like ducks.'

When we get outside, a wall of heat knocks me sideways. Maddie grips my arm. 'Hold up,' she says, fixing her other arm around my waist. 'You're going to have to start eating and sleeping. I can't keep scraping you off the ground.'

I take a few deep breaths to steady myself. 'Why do you think they're back?'

'Those detectives? It's anyone's guess. I wouldn't pin too much on it. They would have told you if they'd found anything. You look like hell. Come on. I'll get Vera to make you a sambo.'

Arm in arm, we walk awkwardly towards the bar. Moni prances on ahead, batting flies away from her face with that scraggy notebook.

Inside, my eyes take a while to adjust. Thin cracks of light seep through the half-shuttered windows, lending the room an underwater feel that makes me think of Georgie in the bath. Once I sit, the dizziness goes away. Five women are propped on tall stools at the far end of the counter. They wave, saying they'll be over in a minute. Their voices bounce off the hollow walls. The red-necked woman is the loudest.

Maddie orders drinks and sets a plate of sandwiches down in front of me. 'Eat up,' she says before going back over to Vera. I watch her dig her hands into her shorts pockets to retrieve her loose change, which she throws on the counter, leaving the linings of her pockets hanging out. I got her to try on a dress of mine once. I'd worn it when I was pregnant with Georgie: hyacinth blue, short sleeves, high waistline. No idea why I brought it with me. When Maddie finally got it on, she flounced around for a while, lifting up the skirt, doing a fine lady impression, all the time knocking back the beer until she broke into song – some Australian number about cakes and buns which sounded vaguely sexual – and then she caught herself in the mirror and that was it; she was doubled over, roaring with laughter, her face wet with tears. She said: *Some Sheila might look awful sharp in this, but it ain't me*. I cut up the dress for dusters after that.

Moni tips the beetle out onto the table. 'Go on,' she says, egging it along. The beetle doesn't move; probably scared to death. I have the urge to crush the damn thing under my thumb. She waits a while and then scoops it back into the matchbox.

'You shouldn't keep it closed in like that. It's cruel,' I tell her. 'Wash your hands before you eat.' She's too busy making notes in her book to reply. Her sketches are quite good, scientific-looking. Michael thinks she's going to be an entomologist.

Maddie sets her beer and my water on the table and slides over the Coke, which I can guarantee Moni will not touch.

'Cheers,' Maddie says, though not in a celebratory way. She flings her head back, taking a deep gulp, wiping her mouth on the sleeve of her man's shirt. 'Why aren't you eating?'

I pick up one of the meat-spread sandwiches to please her.

Maddie holds up her glass and studies the beer. 'I can't really believe that we're leaving. Not that I'll miss the place.' She takes a few gulps.

I keep chewing but it's hard to swallow with the acid taste in my mouth.

'What are you going to do?' Maddie asks.

When I finally manage to down the sandwich, my eyes well up and I blubber like a fool. Moni looks at me vacantly for a moment, then she carries on drawing.

Maddie offers me a paper napkin she has plucked from the metal holder.

'I'm sorry,' I say, blowing my nose.

'What the hell should you be sorry for? For Christ's sake, we've all got our crying to do.' She drinks the rest of her beer and waves her empty glass at the bar.

Vera comes over with another one. 'Might as well get rid of them. We're not going to cart a load of crates with us.' She sets down the glass and scrapes a hand through her short curls, holding a tea-towel in her other hand.

'Cheers,' Maddie says. 'I'll help you clear up later.' She draws the fresh glass towards her.

While Vera mops a spill from the table, she says: 'Our Mr Harvey must be knee-deep for them to repossess like this. Houses aren't much good to the bank out here. It's no wonder they're moving them by the dozen.' She flashes the silver fillings on her bottom back teeth as she yawns. Then she peers over Moni's shoulder at the open book. 'That's brilliant,' she says, narrowing her eyes to see through the watery light. 'I should get you to draw me.' She laughs, a big round ball of a laugh. Maddie laughs too. And when Moni says she's running out of paper, the pair of them start howling like wild dogs. I try to smile, I really do.

Once the laughter dies off, Vera's face stiffens into a series of deep-cut lines. With her cloth stretched out between both hands, she says: 'Had you any idea how much trouble your brother-in-law was in?' Her eyes settle on my shoulder. 'There's probably a lot you don't know about that man.' She is trying to absolve me of any responsibility.

Even so, I resent the way it's said. What I know or don't know about Eddie is none of Vera's business. 'We all make mistakes,' I say.

The two women nod, although they clearly disagree. Which prompts me to add: 'He might be a selfish bastard but he's not a criminal.'

I can feel Moni listening. She makes you think she's busy with her own thing, but I know she's listening and taking note. One day all this will be thrown back in our faces, word for word.

Vera flexes the cloth as she speaks. 'I wasn't suggesting he'd broken the law.'

'Mind you,' Maddie says, 'you don't get that kind of money from chopping wood. I like Mr Harvey. He's been good to us. Jake thinks he's a gentleman. But you have to wonder. That bloody fence would have cost a small fortune, which, evidently, he doesn't have. He's going to be hit for a massive sum of compensation. People won't take this lying down. Removal costs will be the least of it. I feel sorry for him, but in a way he's had it coming for a long time.'

Vera turns to the women at the end of the bar, signalling them over with a flick of her cloth. As they approach, Maddie draws her stool closer to mine. 'Look,' she says, 'I don't know what the hell is going on. The whole thing is a bloody nightmare. What I do know is that a new town like this shouldn't have so many dark corners. If she was here, we would have found her. I'll bet there won't be a sinner left in this town come Sunday. You can't stay.' We both turn to watch Moni stretch out along the bench and close her eyes. The medication must be working. Maddie lowers her voice. 'You know what's funny; I keep remembering things … things I've spent my whole life trying to forget. Do you ever wonder what life would have been like if you'd done something else?'

'Like what?'

'I don't know. Married a different fella.'

'We've all got regrets, if that's what you mean.'

'Course we have. And harping on about them does no one any good.' She drains the last of her beer and stands up to let the other women in around the table. 'We've had a collection, nothing much. Just wanted to give you something to remember us by.' One of the women sets a small brown paper package in front of me. The thin blue ribbon reminds me of a gift Michael gave me on my first night in the country club: a gold-plated watch with my initials carved on the inside. I think I lost it at the swimming pool that summer. I didn't wear one after that, not until Eddie bought me this one last year.

As I look up at these expectant women staring down at me, I get that terrible ache in my chest. I shouldn't have come. It would have been better to wait at the service station until the search is over. I don't want their pity. The red-necked woman, who has an Irish name that is hard to pronounce, says: 'We'd have done the same for anyone. God knows, it's hard enough living in a town like this, without all the heartache.' She sounds like she's reciting lines from a play.

'Sit down,' Maddie says, gesturing to the remaining three before sinking back into her own chair. 'You're making the poor woman nervous.'

A few of them laugh.

'Go on then, open it; it won't bite.' Maddie lifts the package and puts it squarely in my hands. I pull the ribbon loose and tear at the brown paper.

For a few seconds, I just stare at it, and then I say: 'It's beautiful.'

Maddie fastens the inlaid opal bracelet around my wrist. 'There you go,' she says. Then the women put their warm sweaty hands on my skin and squeeze my arms and shoulders.

'You can't go forgetting us now.' Vera laughs.

I hug her. I hug each of them. 'So kind, thank you.' I keep saying thank you. And I mean it. From the bottom of my heart.

'To the Akarula women!' the red-neck says.

We all join in: 'To the Akarula women!' Glasses are raised and chinked in solidarity before the real drinking begins. I float between conversations, catching snippets, moving on before I get involved, keeping my eye on Moni, who is asleep despite the noise. It's amazing how loud seven women can be. At one point I lean in close to Moni's mouth to check she is still breathing.

Three rounds later, the red-neck stands, announcing that she is going to finish packing, and the momentary thread that has bound us together snaps. One by one the women leave. No one knows how to say goodbye.

'Why don't we all go?' Maddie says to those still drinking.

'That's right, desert the sinking ship.' Vera grins and flaps her hands. 'Go on then, bugger off. It's about time I got this lot cleared up. The men will be in soon.'

She clutches an armful of bottles, which clank together tunelessly as she retreats behind the bar. Without another word we gather our things. I jostle Moni awake and follow the others out. Gradually the women separate, each heading off towards their own front door.

'Why don't you wait with me?' Maddie asks, dragging us along the road. Her eyes are heavy with drink; she is no longer able to hold a smile.

'We'll go and meet them,' I say, pulling back. 'Thanks. For everything.'

'Next time,' Maddie says, lurching towards me and clutching my face between her hands. She kisses me on the lips and then kisses Moni's forehead before staggering off towards her house. There won't be a next time.

The heat has fallen out of the day. It is impossible to say how much time has passed. Moni spots the men out on the far side of the Wattle Creek road, small and indistinct from this distance. She says: 'Do you think they've found her?'

I set out towards them, but have to stop and wait for Moni; she's so slow. 'Stop dragging your feet. I'm tired too.' I attempt to lift her and my back gives way. The men are heading towards us; they must have finished. I drag Moni by the arm and walk as fast as I can with this drilling pain at the base of my spine.

Eventually we get close enough to pick out faces from the line of men. I check between their legs for Georgie, even thought I know. Michael trails at the back of the group, and what I think of is that wet stormy day in Whitley Bay when my seven-year-old self got washed out to sea by a freak wave and nearly drowned. A man with a stripy wool scarf swam out and rescued me. He carried me along the promenade. It all happened so quickly, there was no time to be afraid.

Detective Delaney towers head and shoulders above the line. When we are close enough, she signals in her abrupt way. We turn as she approaches and accompany her to the detectives' portacabin, which I thought they had vacated. Moni walks between Delaney and me, clutching her matchbox.

When we are at the door, Delaney explains. 'There are a few papers to sign. I'm sorry.' She's not sorry; she doesn't even try to sound sorry. Michael comes up behind us and rests his hands on Moni's shoulders. He scarcely acknowledges me.

'Where did you go?' I start to say, but he has moved on into the portacabin and my voice bounces off his hard back.

The room is cramped; there is a damp papery smell. I get lodged in a corner behind a plastic table, amidst boxes, which I can only assume contain items found on various searches. The insects get louder as the heat dies away, drowning out any thoughts that try to surface, except one that punches the inside of my head. *She's gone.*

Delaney reaches across the table and takes up a folder, which she hands to Michael. 'I've marked the places where you need to sign.'

Then she pulls down a polythene bag from the shelf above my head and passes me Moni's orange cardigan. I take it out of the bag and press the wool against my cheek; it still smells faintly of Georgie: powdered, musty, eggs on toast. Moni steps out from behind Michael and yanks the cardigan from my hands, and then she puts it on. She stands there in that orange cardigan as if she's making some kind of statement. I have to stop myself from slapping her. I want to scream. I swallow hard; it rises up, again and again, like a surge of vomit, not quite breaking through.

While I'm signing my bit, Eddie comes in looking shattered. I almost feel sorry for him. Detective Walsh is right behind him.

'We're not finished,' Eddie says, staring wildly around the room.

'Sit down.' Delaney offers him one of the flimsy deckchairs. 'We've been over everywhere a dozen times,' she says briskly. 'We're as baffled as you are.'

Baffled? How can she say she is baffled, as if this is a quiz or some crossword puzzle?

'I thought you might have stayed until your job was done,' I say.

'The only option now is to widen the search. We just needed to tie up these loose ends today.' Delaney pulls back her lips, showing off her obtrusive front teeth.

In my rush to get outside, I knock over one of the boxes. I follow the track back across to the street, running until the wire fence stops me. Finally that scream bursts out, taking with it the last shreds of hope, scattering them about like breadcrumbs for those wretched birds to eat.

The remaining houses loom ghostly white against the reddening sky as I make my way back … I was going to say home, but this is not home; it has never been my home. There is nothing that reminds me of what I've done, people I've known, familiar landmarks. Whatever was here before we came is hidden in a mass of rocks and scrub and red brown wilderness that no one cares enough about to name. What was it that Eddie found so captivating about this place?

I get to the caravan without knowing how. Moni and Michael must be over at Eddie's by now. Switching on the light, I stand for a moment, trying to register the changes. There are boxes everywhere, and a suitcase laid out on the bed with clothes flung in randomly. Michael's clothes. Without thinking, I take the clothes out, fold them neatly and repack them. He has crammed some of Georgie's things into a box with Moni's books: toys and shoes, the sponge crocodile Eddie bought her for the bath.

The table is covered with scraps of paper: Michael's notes for his new article. These last few days he's been working on it through the night. With the boxes in the way, I don't see Moni at first; there is so much clutter. Part of her leg shows, just above her knee.

'Moni?' I step over the boxes to get to the table, and bend down to speak to her. 'What are you doing?' She is lying on her back with her arms stretched out by her sides, eyes closed.

'Practising,' she says.

'Practising for what?'

She opens her eyes.

'Get up,' I say. 'The floor's filthy. Where's Dad?'

'He told me to wait here. We're leaving tomorrow. Georgie's dead, isn't she?' She climbs out from underneath the table and sits cross-legged on the cushioned seat opposite me.

'I don't think we'll see her again,' I say, gripping the edge of the table between us.

Moni nods. I do everything in my power not to cry, swallowing over and over until the pain is pushed right down. It's easy to forget that Moni is only eleven. We look across at each other.

'You hungry?' I ask, swallowing again.

'No.'

'Me neither. We should eat something though. Let's go and see what Uncle Eddie has in the fridge.'

We step out into the crisp evening air. It's amazing how quickly the heat disappears once the sun goes down. I keep Moni close to me as we make our way across the tarmac, and then I shout, 'Race you!' running as fast as I can towards the shop. I slow down when I get to the pumps and watch Moni speed past me, her arms flapping as if she is trying desperately to fly.

We fall into the shop breathless, and both collapse against the counter. The shutters are down. After a few heavy breaths, I catch Michael's voice coming from the sitting room.

'Who was it?'

Eddie's there too. 'I don't know. All of them.' He sounds defensive.

'Why the hell didn't you stop them?' Something crashes, a thud; I can't tell what.

'Who is looking after him?' Michael's voice again.

Moni looks at me and whispers, 'Why is Dad shouting?'

I march up to the door and am about to grab the handle when it swings open. Michael stands there, staring wide-eyed at me. Neither of us speaks.

And then Moni steps between us. 'We're going to make some supper. Are you hungry?'

He puts his hand on her head. 'Not now.' Looking at my chin, he says, 'There's been an accident.' His voice is squashed.

I call after him as the door closes. 'What accident?'

The sitting room is a mess, the model town strewn across the floor. The base is broken in two parts. Moni scrabbles around retrieving all the buildings, and attempts to piece the model back together. It will never be the same as it was.

Eddie's voice comes out of nowhere. 'They were like a pack of hyenas.'

I spin round to find him pressed up against the back wall. The sight of him makes me shudder. 'Did Michael hit you?' He is covered in blood and his shirt is torn.

He shakes his head, stuttering: 'I tried to stop them. They wouldn't stop. Kept shouting things, horrible things. They tore him apart.'

I move closer to examine his face. There are no cuts.

'Mr M's in a desperate state,' he says.

It takes me a moment to understand what has happened. 'I'll go and help Michael,' I say, but Eddie bars the door.

'It's not safe. There was too much drink, too much free drink, with the bar closing.'

Mr M's blood is drying on Eddie's face as he leaves.

Moni asks me to explain. I tell her there was a fight, which Uncle Eddie tried to stop. As I go through the door I say, 'It'll be alright.' If she could see my face, she'd know I was lying.

There are days-old dishes piled up in the kitchen sink, breakfast still on the table. I open the fridge and throw out the rotten milk, cheese and sliced ham that hasn't been covered. I make some pasta and stick a plate of sweet biscuits on the tray. Mr M loved my girls, I know he did. How could they think that he would hurt my little girl?

Moni is scribbling in her book when I return with the food. She has managed to piece the model back to its original order. 'The train station is broken,' she says, putting her book down and picking up the small model station.

'Never mind. I doubt there'll be a train station now.' I set the tray on the edge of the table and hand her a plate. Once I taste the pasta, I realise how hungry I am. Moni needs encouragement to eat; I pass her a biscuit, and lean in to read what she has written. *Dad is helping him. He'll be alright. When you come back we can go and visit. You can tell him he is BLAST. He'll like that.* I read on until Moni senses what I'm doing and snaps the book shut.

We play Scrabble, which is probably Moni's favourite game, except for reading words out of the dictionary and guessing their meaning; she is word mad.

'Niobe. Is that a word?' she asks, cocking her head as she examines her letters.

I have to give it to her; the dictionary is in the caravan, and after a few seconds of intense thought, she is convinced it is a word. Can't tell me what it means though.

We are down to the last few letters when Eddie gets back. 'How is he?' I ask, pushing myself up, trying to ignore the pins

119

and needles in my feet. Moni stands too, clutching her letter-holder in her hands.

'We've put him in one of the portacabins. Susan will fly out first thing tomorrow.' There is an odd sense of calm about him.

'Will you watch Moni?' I ask.

Eddie nods. 'It's alright now,' he says, smiling with such a peaceful look on his face.

I will never forget that look.

After taking a torch from the hall cupboard, I head out to the caravan. Michael is round the back, burning rubbish in one of the oil drums.

'Do you think Mr M will be alright?' I ask, startling him. Smoke and darkness distort his face as he carries on slamming rubbish into the drum. I watch the flames lick the sides, moving back to get away from the heat.

When Michael has thrown the last bit of rubbish onto the fire, he asks. 'Are you coming with us?'

Our eyes drive through the smoke. I shake my head, too upset to speak.

'I'm going to finish packing,' he says. 'Why did you let him film you?'

Thoughts come and go but nothing stays long enough for me to form a proper sentence. So Michael heads towards the caravan.

'Wait,' I plead.

He stops. The fire spits and roars with the unexpected breeze. I take a step towards him, staying this side of the oil drum. 'Do you hate me?' I ask. My whole body is trembling.

Michael talks the way he talks into his Dictaphone. 'Moni and I are leaving tomorrow, if the pilot gets back, or else the day after. If we ever find Georgie, it won't be here. You know that as well as I do.'

'What do you mean?'

'Moni doesn't want to stay here.'

I stare at him, trying to make sense of it all. 'We can't give up.'

'It's not about giving up,' he says.

'Would you really leave without me?'

He doesn't answer. A large brown moth hovers about the flames. Michael tries to bat it away but it comes back; there is a faint hissing sound as it catches fire.

I shoot past him into the caravan and pick up the first box I find, flinging it through the open door, then I throw out the next one and the next. He tries to stop me, wrestling a box of books out of my hands. I snatch some clothes from the suitcase and stuff them through the window, lunging for another box before Michael pins my arms to my sides. He pulls me into him; my back presses up against his chest. His breath warms the nape of my neck.

'Calm down,' he says, still holding me.

I laugh and cry at the same time, overwhelmed by the absurdity of it all. His grip slackens, but he doesn't let go. His body feels warm where his skin touches mine. I inch my legs back so that my calves touch his legs, just for a second. I can feel the hem of his shorts through my dress, against my thighs. His arms drop.

'Don't let go,' I whisper, staying where I am.

Feeling his hand against my thigh, I search for his other hand and pull it around me, planting it onto my stomach. Slowly he turns me round. I run my fingers over his hair and down his face, as if I am blind, as if this will help me remember what is now completely lost. As my fingers travel over his lips, he bites them.

I slap him so hard, my hand burns. He doesn't move until I go for him again, and then he lunges at me while I kick and punch.

He defends himself, grappling with me as our joint weight casts us to the floor. I lose track of where my arms and legs are, our limbs flail about so much. We keep moving and resisting each other; each time we pull apart, we get closer. And the smell, our smell, wet, frowzy, mildew, covers everything. My dress gets torn. Grit from the floor wedges in my back. Eventually we shed our clothes and cling onto each other, battling through sex as if we were at war, losing ourselves until we both surrender. And for a second I see Eddie. I feel Eddie. Then just at the moment Michael's body goes rigid against mine, I tell him, 'I love you.' He opens his eyes and stares at me in disbelief.

After that, he pulls away and lies by my side. Our hands barely touch; our bodies stiffen like two river logs, already drifting apart. He turns to face the wall. I watch his back for a while before pulling on my dress, which is now missing three buttons. Taking a cigarette from my bag, I prop myself against the caravan door and light up, finding the smoke vaguely reassuring. The petrol pumps look like headless soldiers reflected in the faint moonlight.

The bed creaks as Michael gets up. He moves about the caravan. I don't look to see what he's doing until he presents me with a sandwich on a piece of kitchen towel. He's made one for himself.

'I've told Moni we're leaving tomorrow,' he says, sitting on the edge of the bed, talking between mouthfuls.

I put the sandwich down beside me and continue to look out past the service station. At night the bush comes alive, as if it is breathing. 'I know she's not alive. But we have to find her. We can't just abandon her.' I talk and think and talk, not knowing which is which.

Michael says, 'I'm not suggesting we leave the country. I just know she isn't here.'

'How do you know?'

'It's Moni you should think about.'

He crosses over to the table and sits down on the cushioned bench. Using his teeth, he pulls off the top of his pen and starts to write.

I stub out my cigarette on the step and pick up the sandwich, dusting off the ants. There are suddenly so many ants. The crumbs get attacked as soon as they hit the floor. After putting the kettle on, I wipe the surfaces while I'm waiting, watching the army of ants troop across the steps. I pour boiling water on them, scattering them like shrapnel; some get swept along in the tide, a warning to other unsuspecting ants. My father always said, if you don't wipe them out straight away, they'll take over.

'I'm going to check on Moni. I'll sleep on the settee tonight,' I say.

Michael grunts and shrugs, making that annoying clicking sound with his false tooth. I snatch the torch off the draining board and hesitate long enough to realise that I am hoping he will say something. He doesn't even look up.

I cross the tarmac, ignoring the rising panic in my chest, in my throat; it won't go away. I creep through the shop into the hall. The lights are out and the sitting-room door is open. Moni mumbles in her sleep: a low persistent drone. I stand at the end of the camp bed and watch her. Whatever she is dreaming plays itself out in her body as if she were awake. I want to wake her up, to hear her voice, to tell her something, anything. Instead, I rearrange her sheet and lightly touch her cheek.

In Eddie's office, I run my hands across the wall, feeling the small lumpy contours where the plasterer got lazy. Why do we need walls? What are we so afraid of? That someone will come and knock them down, that without them we'll be exposed to each other as we really are? Is it just that we all need a place to hide?

I poke my head around Eddie's bedroom door. 'Eddie?' There's no answer. The blinds are drawn; it is completely dark. 'Are you awake?'

I just want to hear a voice, any voice except my own. My mind keeps throwing out the blackest thoughts. I creep back through the office, the sitting room, and tiptoe down the hall. I close the bathroom door behind me. The toilet seat feels refreshingly cold through my dress as I sit. Turning on the radio, I let the air fill up with chatter: soft drawling voices that lull me to sleep. I sleep awake on the toilet, not knowing whether my eyes are open or closed.

The sun is gushing through the window when Moni pushes open the door.

'What are you doing?' she asks, stepping up to the sink, pinching her toothbrush between her fingers.

'I must have fallen asleep. What time is it?'

'Uncle Eddie's gone.'

'Gone where?'

'To get Georgie.'

She turns on the tap but there is no water. 'See if the kitchen taps work,' I say, getting up and stretching my legs, which have gone stiff. My neck is killing me. I switch off the radio and follow Moni through to the kitchen. She spits the toothpaste froth onto the dishes in the sink. These taps don't work either. 'He's probably gone to fix the water. Let's go and find Dad. He might have made breakfast. You never know.' I give her a bit of undiluted orange squash to wash away the taste.

Today must be the hottest day on record, despite the swelling clouds. The melted tarmac sticks to our flip flops, making it hard to walk. Flies attempt to feed off our sweat. I hate these flies. I hate that rotten caravan. I hate feeling like I'm being barbecued.

Eddie's truck has gone. (I never asked him what he did with that kangaroo.)

Moni points at the galahs lined up on the telegraph wire. 'Shall we feed them?'

'Your dad might have fed them already.' As we approach the caravan, I say, 'This looks like a good place for breakfast. What do you think?'

I see myself playing waitress to Moni and Michael as they peer at invisible menus. How could I have risked losing the most important thing? Moni raps on the door and calls out, 'Is this café open?' She marches in. I'm right behind her.

Everything is packed, except for the pictures I bought in Wattle Creek, and the drawings Moni and Georgie made of Mr M. I check the cupboards and the wardrobe. My clothes are still hanging up, but the rest have gone.

'I'll go and find him,' Moni says, ripping the pictures and drawings down, leaving them on the table before she darts outside.

'You can't go on your own. It's not safe,' I call after her, but she has started running. I try to follow but my legs buckle under me. 'Come back,' I shout, struggling to stand. I watch her shrinking as my eyelids flicker.

The sweat on my skin turns cold. And all I can see is miles and miles of empty space.

MICHAEL

I am driving – Akarula Street shrinks in the rear-view mirror as I head towards Wattle Creek – slow driving, curling round potholes and sharp gullies. Being behind the wheel again feels like running with my eyes closed; anything could happen.

The sun bounces off the road in waves of silvery white light. It's the light that makes the ground seem to roll up in dusty folds of terracotta. I can hardly tell the earth from the sky. Through the rear-view mirror I check on Mr M, who is sprawled across the back seat. He winces every time we hit a bump. His face is disfigured with bruises, one of his eyes too swollen to open.

Around 5am Eddie hammered on the caravan window, shouting in a way that made me think he'd found Georgie. I was half-asleep, so what he said didn't register until afterwards. He practically dragged me outside and over to the truck. I was still dressed from the day before. It wasn't until we were almost at the portacabin that I fully understood.

'I can't get through to the hospital,' Eddie said. 'The line's engaged.' His face was blanched and he was shivering. 'Susan isn't answering. If we wait, it'll be too late.' There was panic in his voice. I'd never seen him so shaken up.

When we got to the portacabin door, Eddie rushed past me. Mr M was choking and coughing blood.

'Look at him,' Eddie screeched.

The great Edward Harvey was losing control, flailing his arms about as if he was drowning. 'Can you hear us?' he shouted into Mr M's face, like some bad actor in a sitcom.

I wanted to say something about Father, about why he left us that way, but I didn't know exactly how to start, and the moment passed before I could find the right words. Eddie has Father's eyes.

'Calm down,' is what I offered.

I propped Mr M up with a pillow so that he could clear his throat. Then I knelt beside the bed and tried to get him to tell us what was happening, but his mouth was badly cut and when his lips parted, all that came out was spit and blood.

Eddie squatted on the floor beside me, holding his hand an inch from Mr M's cheek. After a while he drew back and seemed to be praying. Or cursing. At any rate, his hands were clasped and he was mumbling like an idiot. For a second, I didn't recognise him. My proud cock-and-bull brother wouldn't kneel at someone's feet, not the invincible Eddie. Whether he read my thoughts, or whether the pain of losing himself to a higher cause got too much, I don't know, but within seconds he was pushing himself up. He started trying to fix the faulty door catch.

'Some bastard's got it in for me,' he said, rattling the catch the way a child might shake a broken toy.

'For you?' It was almost amusing under the circumstances.

We carried Mr M out to the truck and laid him on the back seat. He kept convulsing. We almost dropped him twice. Eddie wore this manic look, the whites of his eyes taking over his whole face as he ranted about Akarula and the mine, not making any sense.

'You'll have to drive,' I said. 'Just try the hospital again. It won't be easy for him being stuck in the car for five hours.' I didn't say what I was thinking, but I could see Eddie being stranded on a deserted road in the middle of nowhere with a dead man on the back seat.

'Mike?' Eddie clung onto the top of the truck door as I got in the back with Mr M. 'Is it too late?'

I had no time for his theatricals, so I yanked at the door and told him to get a move on.

While he was gone, I stretched forwards between the seats and played with the radio dial, surfing the stations to get a decent reception. I talked about God knows what, to hold Mr M's attention, to stop him from closing his one good eye. Eddie wasn't long. I heard him racing back across the tarmac.

'They said it'll be quicker to drive. You'll have to drive.' He was panting and holding his side as if he was in pain.

'I can't.' But I could see he wasn't in a fit state to do anything. He could hardly breathe. And so I rearranged Mr M on the back seat, belting his body in as best I could, and climbed into the driver's seat. Eddie swam in the tail lights as I pulled out onto the road. It's nearly six years since I sat behind a wheel. *I could have killed that boy.*

The smell of sun-baked rocks coats the warm breeze, hitting my face as I wind down the window. With Akarula behind me, I can sense the boundless expanse Eddie talked about: no walls, no borders, no houses, just miles and miles of arid bush. I drive past colossal termite mounds, memorials to the primacy of insects. The cracked red earth looks shell-like. Georgie has fallen down one of these cracks. Whatever we do now will not bring her back.

Without warning, the shine slips out of the sun. I sense the familiar void descending on me. How can you wake up one day and feel as if the earth is being smothered by the sky? It wasn't even like that; it wasn't one day. It crept up on me, this overwhelming feeling of pointlessness; there was no way of dodging it. Believe me, I tried. I did everything I could. It just got worse and worse.

I press the throttle down, faster, as fast as the rutted dirt road will allow, stirring the surface dust, covering my tracks. I force myself to breathe. We should be there by eleven at this rate.

'How are we doing back there?' I ask, peering at Mr M through the rear-view mirror as he closes and opens his good eye. What does he make of all this? He tried warning us, told me weeks ago that people were getting restless, that it was time for us to go. It must have been a few days before Georgie disappeared. I didn't know what he was talking about. He laughed when I asked him if he'd read it in the stars. But he knew. At the time I remember thinking *he's right, we should go.* I told Caroline.

I drive along this endless road for hours. Near Wattle Creek, the surface improves, turning into bitumen a few miles out of town. Wattle Creek is roughly the same size as Alice Springs. There is one main shopping street, but the houses sprawl in all directions.

'Alright, Mr M? We'll have you in a proper bed in no time.'

He presses his hands into the seat. If he's trying to lift himself, he makes no headway. Still, he's alive. And we're nearly there.

The drive through this plain, dusty, ten-horse town takes all of three minutes. I pull up in front of the hospital, a grey building with two portacabins to the side.

'I'll fetch a helper,' I say. 'Won't be long.'

He nods. No, he doesn't nod; he shifts his head slightly, and winces with pain. I nod, slamming the truck door, and sprint towards the entrance.

There's a reception area in the small foyer. I press the brass bell on the desk. It's a little after eleven. A nurse arrives, the same one we had the last time I was here with Moni, although she doesn't seem to recognise me.

'My brother rang this morning,' I explain. 'I'll need help getting my friend inside. Is Susan here?'

This young, severe-looking woman whose hair is scraped back in a high ponytail, picks her nail as she responds. 'Doctor Marshall's on a call at the moment. Why don't you take a seat while we get your friend inside?' She gives me a form to fill in, offering a pen from her top pocket. 'As soon as she arrives, I'll let her know you're here.' She accelerates down the corridor in her plain white pumps. A few minutes later, two male hospital workers carry Mr M past me on a stretcher.

My arms get chicken skin from the air-conditioning, which circulates the smell of disinfectant. I study the pictures of hand-painted fruit trees on the wall behind the desk: simple drawings done by an amateur. The nurse appears again with a cup of coffee and a snack pack of digestive biscuits.

'I'm afraid we've no waiting room,' she says. 'They're supposed to be building one next year, but who knows.' A curt smile before she marches back down the corridor, disappearing behind the swing doors.

I fill out the form and wait in one of the chairs lined up along the wall. My mind wanders in and out. Is it an apple tree or a pear tree? The frame needs straightening. If Mr M dies, people will assume he was guilty. *God saves the innocent.* I've heard that phrase uttered I don't know how many times lately. Like when they used to drown witches; without your superhuman powers, you wouldn't survive. What does it all mean? I'm not a religious man. As far as I'm concerned, the church is nothing more than a powerhouse built to instil fear in the common people. Still, I've tried praying. Maybe praying would have helped, if I'd believed, if I'd had an ounce of faith. Caroline encourages the girls to pray. What if He *is* up there? That's her argument. She's not really a believer either, but she keeps a foot in both camps just in case.

I don't know what happened last night: we fought like animals, and then, throughout the sex, it was as if she had gone, deserted her own skin; I couldn't feel her. I loved that woman. I wanted to be the one to make her happy. Of course you can't *make* someone happy, not really, but you can try. She was, she still is, the best thing that ever happened in my life, despite how we've turned out. Her and the girls. My whole world in three females. But I keep seeing that tape, replaying it; I can't seem to rub it out.

A while later, a voice cuts through my thoughts.

'Michael?' Susan rests her hand on my shoulder as she looks down at me. The lines around her eyes multiply as she smiles.

'Have you seen him? Will he be alright?' I ask.

'He's not good. A bruised liver, fractured ribs that are threatening to puncture a lung. At the moment he's in a critical state. You did the right thing bringing him in. Sorry we couldn't get out to you. It's a long drive. You must be exhausted.'

'What can I do?'

'Get some rest.' She studies my face as if she's searching underwater for the remains of a sunken boat.

As I stand, the empty biscuit wrapper falls from my lap. Both of us bend down to pick it up.

'Mr Markarrwala is in good hands,' she says, putting the wrapper in the bin behind the desk, moving with surprising grace. 'You're not thinking of driving back today, are you? There's a spare room in my house if you need somewhere to stay. I promised Eddie I'd look after you.'

'We're supposed to be flying to Adelaide.'

'Today?' She gives me a wry smile. 'You can rearrange your flight from my house, if you like. When was the last time you slept?' She pushes her light fringe back off her face and sticks one hand in her trouser pocket.

I no longer care what we do.

'You're moving out then?' she asks.

'I've rented a place, until we can find something decent. The Adelaide *Advertiser* has agreed to take me on part-time, bits and pieces, but it should be enough to tide us over.'

'That's great.' She scratches the side of her nose as she says, 'I heard there was some kind of evacuation going on.'

'They closed the mine.'

'I know. Let me make you some lunch at least. I've got a break now, and you'll not get far on an empty stomach.' She heads off, signalling with a tilt of her head for me to follow. And I do, like a dog on a lead.

Her green Datsun is parked a few yards from the door.

'The house is only five minutes away,' she calls over her shoulder.

In the car she changes her shoes for some open-toed sandals, slinging the other pair in the back.

'Did Eddie tell you what happened?' I ask, watching her tug the gear stick into neutral and start the engine.

'Is he alright? I hardly recognised him on the phone.'

She turns to watch me as I speak. 'He saw the whole thing. Women too, using their fists. We called the police.'

'I suspect an old aboriginal man won't stir up too much excitement. You'll be lucky if they bother coming out. How's Monica?'

'Sleeping better, thank God.'

Nodding, she releases the hand brake and starts driving. 'It's going to take time. There are no quick fixes. It obviously doesn't help that Georgina still hasn't been found.'

The cooling fans take effect as we drive down the main street: wooden buildings mostly, shop fronts, wide glass windows, advertising billboards, nondescript faces, working clothes. I understand that we may never know what happened to Georgie. I understand, but I don't accept – we went through every tunnel, combed every inch of ground.

Susan pulls off the main road, stopping outside a one-storey house.

'This is it. I'm hardly ever here, so excuse the mess. Not the house-proud type.' She pats the dashboard before getting out. 'I do shift work with the flying doctors, and between that I pretty much live at the hospital.'

'Busy woman.'

'Something like that.'

The heat falls in on me as soon as I open the door. Susan plucks at her blouse to let the air in, revealing her plain white bra. She's not overtly feminine, not in the way she dresses anyway, but there is something distinctly womanly about her.

'We could do with some rain to break the humidity. The weather man said it's on its way.' She wipes her forehead with the back of her hand as she speaks.

She is slim, natural-looking; a dark magnetism sits about her eyes. As she unlocks the front door, I catch the scent of her hair, cedar or beech, uncombed, roughly cut, pushed back in a way that suggests she doesn't care.

The living room is barren: hardly any furniture and no books or ornaments to speak of. Everything is purely functional. She offers me one of the wooden chairs stranded by the window.

'I'll see what's in the fridge,' she says.

I survey the room as I talk to her through the kitchen door. 'How long have you known Eddie?'

'Four years. We were one of the first couples to move to Akarula. My partner, John, was working for Lansdowne Corporation. He helped set up the mine, sorted the business end of things. Eddie probably told you.'

'I forgot you had a partner.' I shift the chair slightly so that I can see her padding around the kitchen in her bare feet. She sets a tray with cutlery and plates and a selection of food.

'We planned to get back to Sydney by Christmas – it was never our intention to stay – and then one of the mine shafts collapsed.

They hadn't secured it properly. John died the next day. Your brother was so good; flew here every week to check that I was alright. He knew John pretty well.' She hesitates as if she's going to say more but then changes tack. 'Do you like cheese?'

I nod as she looks through the doorway at me.

'Is your family from here?' I want to understand why she stays in this town.

'Sydney. I didn't have the heart to go back on my own. Our life was here. Sometimes I wake up expecting to see him. Four years and I can still fool myself.' She pauses, holding a loaf of bread between her hands, and looks down at the worktop as she says, 'We'd just started trying for a baby.'

She turns back to face me, registering, with a slight blush, that I've been watching her. 'Sorry, I didn't mean to tell you all that.'

'I'm glad you did.'

Her face softens into smooth silk lines that open up a new aspect. After putting on the kettle, she says, 'He's a good man, your brother. I'll miss him.'

'He's not going anywhere.'

'No?' I get up and help her with the tray, setting it on the table. 'With the mine closed,' she says 'there won't be enough people left to make it worthwhile sending supplies. He can't stay there on his own.'

'You don't know Eddie.' But maybe she does?

She lifts off the bread, a plate of cold meats and cheese, an assortment of jams, and props the tray up against the wall.

'How's Caroline?'

I want to tell her, only what would I say? *Caroline and Eddie had sex.*

Susan cuts a slab of bread as she talks. 'You can leave stuff here if you want, until you get settled, save paying for two planes. I never use that back room. And there's a fairly cheap removal man; well, he's the man with the van in Wattle Creek, but he'll do anyone a favour. I can ask him, if you like?'

'Thanks.' I don't know why she is helping me.

She makes coffee. Steam fogs up her glasses as she pours. She uses the sleeve of her blouse to wipe the lens clean. What was her relationship with Eddie? As far as I know, my brother's never managed to be friendly with a woman without taking her to bed.

'Did you finish your article?' she asks, cupping her hands around the sugar pot. She looks different without her glasses on, more accessible.

'Yesterday. They're putting it in the weekend supplement as a cover story.'

'Congratulations.'

'It might help, once more people know.'

We eat in a comfortable silence. Susan stares through the window at the street, her eyelashes catching the sunlight. I pick up her glasses and fiddle with them, making some comment about my father's poor sight. It feels as if she understands everything; there is no need for words. I finish my coffee, savouring the bitter aftertaste, and push my plate to one side.

'Why are you looking at me like that?' she asks.

'You remind me … of someone.' Not someone; she reminds me of the collared dove that used to perch on our crab apple tree and sing for its mate, the mate who never came. Every day for weeks it would sing as if today was the day. I think collared doves are one of those birds who mate for life. I could be wrong. 'I should get going. It's a long drive,' I say, getting up and clearing the plates.

'I'll give Larry a call – see if he's available. Leave those. You've still got time.'

She's right. I do have time. Right now it seems as if I have all the time in the world. I listen to her making arrangements for me on the phone in the hall. Her voice holds the weight of water, clear and refreshing.

As she takes a dirty cup from my hand, she says: 'You'd better cancel that flight to Adelaide. Larry said he can fetch your things on Thursday, if that suits.'

I thank her and lift the tray through to the kitchen. Then I rearrange the flight for Friday.

'Who looks after you?' I ask when I get back into the kitchen.

She presses her earlobe between her fingers, tilting her head as she slowly smiles. 'You think I need looking after?'

I lean back against the sink and gaze at her, really take her in: her face, her hair, her chest, her golden skin. She opens out like a flower, getting pinker as she reaches for her sandals, and balances on one leg to pull them on.

I follow her to the car.

'I'll let you know how Mr Markarrwala is doing,' she says, as I get in beside her. She taps the dashboard again.

We drive back to the hospital, parking beside the truck.

She gets out and says, 'Safe journey. Give my love to Eddie. You know, you probably saved that man's life.' She sticks out her hand. I take hold of it, and we keep holding on until finally her hand slips out of mine. I watch her cross the few yards up to the hospital doors.

When I climb into the truck and start the engine, her face lingers for a while, growing fainter as I drive away. It's almost one o'clock. I'm glad to get out onto the dirt road. I drive for several hours, letting the bareness of the bush wash through me. I think about the girls. I see them together, Moni holding Georgie's hand. I have a conversation with Susan, telling her about Eddie and Caroline. I imagine her response, her eyes, her mouth not quite closed. And then suddenly I am back with those Alsatians, walking in a straight line so as not to miss an inch, calling Georgie in different pitches, remembering all the times I've called her name before: *tea's ready*; *bath's ready*; *time to go*; *Doctor Sutton has arrived*. I didn't want her to hear that I was frightened, so I tried to make her name sound reassuring; I needed her to know that wherever she was, she would be alright. Some days I succeeded, others not. Did she hear me? When we crawled through the shafts, feeling the ground for clues, I was terrified that I would find her body. Horrible images etched themselves on my mind: her skin burnt off, her eyes picked out by birds. I didn't want to find her that way. Can you understand? I was afraid of finding her.

Eventually I manage to push these thoughts away and focus on the road ahead, a road that repeats itself endlessly. After another hour, I pull over to stretch my legs, empty my bladder, give my eyes a break. I stop the truck a few yards from one of the termite mounds – incredible structures: a family of several million termites serving one another harmoniously within a tight pecking order. I walk over to the mound, a reddish brown tower of earth, more than twice my height, and run my hands down the sides, feeling the crusted outer layer. How long does it take for them to build one of these? With a small stick, I work a hole into the crust. A few angry soldier ants appear, gnashing their jaws (you can tell they are soldiers by the size of the jaw). Within seconds they have blocked the hole. I pee against the mound before heading back to the truck. In the boot, I search amongst Eddie's tackle for some water. Georgie had water. How much, I don't know.

The waning sun cuts through the windscreen as I drive on. I stick my left hand into my pocket and pull out a packet of pills. These last few days, I've been forgetting to take them. With one hand on the wheel, I pop a pill from the foil wrapping and drop it on my tongue. As soon as the acrid taste coats my mouth, I spit it out. I grab the whole packet and fling them through the window. And I keep driving, slowly letting go.

On the edge of twilight, Akarula emerges out of nowhere, like the Emerald City. The fence looms large against the darkening sky. As I drive towards the steel gates, I notice something on the road. It's hard to see from this distance, with the play of light and shadow. I make out what looks like a large bird – a large bird that turns into a figure, a child. The wheels turn underneath me and my feet work the pedals, but I am no longer aware of driving. I can see Georgie, like a soft dancing flame. I strain my eyes, afraid to breathe in case I blow her out. The closer I get, the more unmistakable she becomes. And then, between blinks, she is gone. Moni takes her place, swinging her arms by her sides as she walks down the middle of the road. I stop the car right in front of her, dropping my forehead against the steering wheel. Moni's voice comes in through the open window.

'Found you,' she says, matter-of-factly.

'What are you doing out here? Where's Mum?' I concentrate on her freckled throat, trying to retrieve the sight of Georgie. She was there, right in front of me, swinging her arms.

'I thought you'd gone. Mum thought so too because she said I wouldn't find you.'

I lean across the passenger seat and open the door. Moni walks around the bonnet and climbs in beside me.

'Where did you go?' She links her hands on her lap as I kiss her forehead. 'Are we still going to Adelaide?'

'I took Mr M to hospital.'

'Is he sick?'

I look at her as I search for the right thing to say. 'He got caught in a fight.'

She nods, frowning. She has a permanent frown – we all do – from too much sun. I hug her tightly. She feels so incredibly small. 'How did you manage to walk this far?'

'When are we leaving?' she asks as she pulls a matchbox out of her pocket and shows me a metallic-green beetle, most likely a Carab.

'Friday. Where did you find this little beauty?' (Moni looks nothing like Georgie. It *was* Georgie I saw.)

'Under a rock. I had to dig it out.' My daughter purses her lips, examining me intently.

We drive the last few miles into Akarula, through the open fence gates, past the last two remaining houses in the street, and Mr M's tree. I've made good time; I didn't think I'd get back before dark. As we round the bend and park up beside the pumps, exhaustion hits. Moni gets out, coming around to my side of the truck. She draws me across the tarmac to the caravan where I collapse on the bed and close my eyes. Almost immediately I drift into a weightless sleep, half-hearing the sounds outside, thoughts merging into each other and dissolving, my body sinking further and further, until the gunshot.

Instinctively I cover my head as another shot is fired. I leap to my feet and fling the door open in time to see the windscreen of Eddie's truck implode. Caroline keeps firing randomly. Two more shots and the tyres go down. As she gets closer, she fires at the bonnet and the boot, putting a hole straight through the back window. Amazingly, the glass remains intact.

'What are you doing?' I shout between shots. She ignores me or doesn't hear. Her face is swollen from crying.

The galahs have taken off in fright and flap around in confused circles. Caroline hooks the rifle skywards and fires again. One of the birds, the smallest, drops to the ground. I look over to Moni, who is crouching beside the petrol pumps, her face stiff with fear, her arms bound tightly around her legs. I head towards her, but then Caroline drops the rifle. Instinctively I turn back and sprint over to the bird. I stoop down and gather up its fragile body; the pink and grey wings seem to fade as its life-force seeps out.

When I look up, my wife is staring at me, her eyes stretched wide, looking truly broken, and old, incredibly old, in the last splash of light.

'I thought you'd gone,' she says. 'Why did you do that?'

Without a word, I straighten up, still holding the galah, and offer it to her. She takes it in both hands.

'Promise you won't leave me here,' she pleads.

I promise; what else can I do?

'Where were you?' she asks.

'In Wattle Creek. Eddie should have told you.'

Something inside me falls over as I stand there watching Caroline cradle that galah like a new-born, the same way she held Moni for the first time, afraid and incredulous.

I pick up the abandoned rifle on my way towards the shop. The shaft is still warm. Where did she learn to shoot like that? After fifteen years, she still surprises me. Moni remains wedged beside the pumps.

'It's alright, love,' I say. 'It's over now.'

The next morning I wake up alone in the caravan. It feels like a prison cell now that the walls have been stripped. I need to finish things with Eddie before we go. One of us has to tell the truth. In six years we've never talked about what happened with Father. I don't suppose we'll ever really know.

The air is thick and lifeless as I walk over to the service station. It's a relief to get inside again. A dusty light coats the shelves of the shop, giving the impression of abandonment: the way we cover up furniture in a disused room, the way when people die we close them in a box because we can't bear to see what is no longer there. I'd give anything for one last glimpse of my daughter.

I drag the curtains open in the sitting room. 'Eddie?' What will he do when everyone's gone?

The room is spotless. My brother's famous model town is positioned centrally on the table, each building exactly in its place; he must have used a ruler to get that straight a line down the street. The broken base has been glued in two parts. As I look at the model, it strikes me that Eddie has never really grown up.

I go through to the office. The pile of papers on his desk has gone. Detailed plans of Akarula are pinned up on the wall; he has circled in red ink the buildings that are yet to be built. The rest of his life is a mess, but the model town and these plans are perfectly ordered.

'Eddie?' With the butt of the rifle I knock on the bedroom door before going in. I hook the handle of the rifle over my shoulder and lift the blinds. Moni's outside, not far from Eddie's truck, holding the dead bird in her hands. She's talking to it, her palm spread flat under its beak. I shouldn't have fed those birds. Caroline was right. If they'd been wilder, they would have flown off with the first shot.

There is a glass of partly drunk whiskey on the window ledge: Eddie's. I knock it back. It burns my throat; I feel it coursing through my body. My eyes water as I wait for the burning sensation to stop. The look on her face while he was filming her, while she was buttoning up her blouse. She doesn't like being in front of a camera, always hated photographs. Why did he film her like that? Some days I look at Caroline and feel as if I am seeing her for the first time.

Resting the rifle on the desk, I stare at the certificate of Land

Purchase nailed to the wall and try to figure out where Eddie might be. The best place to start seems to be the street.

Moni has gone when I get outside. I walk through the bare silence towards the bend. Without the rev of an engine, car radios or talk, the whole place seems dead, deader still now that the fence excludes most of the wildlife. I presumed he was going to fence off the old mine; we all did. It was the obvious choice. Instead he fenced in the whole town. Had this idea that we'd be safer that way. Safe from what? He always takes things too far.

When we were children, Eddie and I used to play shoe-cars. I'd be about six this day I'm thinking of, which would make Eddie three. We were revving our shoes around the carpet, beeping horns, the whole lot, and then we got to a supermarket and Eddie's shoe changed into the shopping trolley and we started loading up. Mother called us from downstairs. I stuck my shoes on. Eddie didn't know what to do. He told me he wasn't going to put a shopping trolley on his foot. Things always stuck too long with him; he could never quite let go.

We made a pact in our early teens to get each other out of trouble, a do or die sort of deal. Small things. I saved him from getting a beating for swearing at the milkman by telling Father I had dared him to. He gave me his post office savings when I lost Mother's purse and had to pay back the contents. Our parents blamed him for the house fire, made him swear he'd never take another photograph. He took his camera everywhere. Drove people mad. Stored his negatives in cardboard boxes in the landing cupboard, which was where the fire started. That's why he bought the cine-camera. I helped him with that too. We both agreed that moving pictures didn't count. We stuck by each other, mainly to protect our own backs. People called us the Harvey Brothers. We were unstoppable. And then I turned fourteen, and somehow the age difference started to matter. I was older and responsible; I didn't want to play his childish games.

If I could, would I get him out of this hole he has dug himself? The answer is no. Edward Harvey can take care of himself. He'll talk his way out of it, just like he's done a dozen times before, and then he'll move on to the next project, never admitting that he failed. Eddie doesn't fail, he just moves on. Although it won't be easy this time.

I follow the road round to the street, searching the bush for a solitary figure. There is no one. There is no street either. A removal truck is waiting outside the store with a crane-like arm moving into place. There is a second truck parked behind it. I didn't think they'd take the store until the very end. This must be the end. How can a town just disappear? I think about Mr M as I go past the ghost gum tree, his tree, its branches spread out like fingers.

A blue Chevrolet is parked outside the last house. A balding man – I forget his name, Queeny's husband – comes out of the house carrying a duffel bag, and throws me a greeting as he walks towards the car, dumping his bag down beside the back wheel. He pumps my hand up and down. 'Well, this is it. All the best.' He starts to say something else but gives up, sighing instead. I want to ask him if he joined in the fight, if he made one of those bruises on Mr M's face, only I haven't got the nerve.

'Have you seen Eddie?' I ask.

'He was heading towards the mine this morning. We were planning to leave first light. The wife got travel sick fifty yards down the road. She's psyching herself up for the journey right now. Whenever she's ready…' He taps the roof of the car several times before walking back towards the house. 'By the way,' he says, turning momentarily, 'There's no water. You might tell Eddie. Not that it matters now, I suppose.'

I nod and wave, realising that I didn't really know any of these people.

Outside what was the general store there are still tubs of flowers, shrivelling now, dead or dying. The limp leaves of the Devil's Tail look like large drops of blood. And the mini gardens, patches of grass fronting the ghost houses, watered every day at one stage, now yellowy-brown. It won't be long before it all gets subsumed into the monotonous bush.

There is a slight breeze, and five iron clouds in the sky. I can feel rain in the air as I turn onto the track that leads out to the mine. Eddie took us on the grand tour of this mine when we first arrived, introduced us to everyone. We went down a shaft. Jake showed us how to tap into the rock. It took all of five minutes before claustrophobia set in. (Those drugs have untold side-effects.) Moni didn't like it much either. The two of us came out and waited for the others to surface. Caroline found a small chip of opal, which caused Eddie to crack open a bottle of champagne. She fell for it, hook, line and sinker – the illusion. Eddie conjured up this illusion and she believed the whole thing.

Me: I'm a servant of facts. My job is to uncover the illusions. But I've come to understand that nothing is more fantastic, more beyond the bounds of belief, than the actual facts. I'm telling you what happened as it happened, trying not to cloud things with opinions and perspectives. In the end, that's all I can do.

Caroline once told me that I had no imagination. I remember the exact day, the time, what I was wearing (jeans and an earthy brown v-neck jumper.) I remember the way she looked at me, with undisguised contempt. I forget now what I was supposed to have done. She said *how can you hope to change the world if you can't imagine something different?* At the time, I didn't understand what she meant. I felt vaguely sorry for her, blinded, as I saw it, by her childish fantasies. Later that evening (there were three stars in the sky) she told me she was pregnant; in the same breath, she asked me if I minded calling the baby Monica, after her mother, if it was a girl. That's when I really understood about changing worlds. Nothing had changed and yet everything was utterly different.

Eddie always wanted to change the world, to be the big man. He's got himself into some shit this time; people are suing. He gave them all a rosy contract, an overindulgent incentive scheme and then didn't deliver. For once in his life, he might just have to reap what he has sown.

The fence is impressive up close, thick meshed wire with two steel girders running diagonally between the posts. I approach the gates that mark the entrance to the mine, passing the water tank on my right. Just past the gates, I see a large animal lying on its side, partly hidden by scrub grass. When I get close, I discover it's a pregnant kangaroo, still warm. I press my hand onto her swollen stomach; there's a faint pulse – the joey inside her is still alive. Since there is nothing I can do, I carry on. People drive like fury along these tracks.

The mine is roughly three miles of open cuts and shafts, exposed where the top layer of sandstone has been blown off. There is plenty of machinery: puddlers, jack hammers, drills, windlasses, all standing idle. When we were having our tour, Jake explained what they did. I couldn't tell you now. What I do know is that it will take a long time for this land to recover.

I turn off the main track towards the portacabins. Just before I reach the first one, I spot something glinting in the dust. After brushing away the surface gravel, I find a huge chunk of opal, about the size of Georgie's hand. I hold it up against the rising sun, the marine greens and blues swim into each other and shine iridescently. Not knowing what else to do, I slip it into my pocket. Some of the miners in this town have made a fortune. A percentage of their finds goes to the company, but the more they hit upon, the more they make. Jake was telling me that on the field a piece of rough opal might be worth anything from $50,000 upwards. Once it's cut and polished you're talking $150,000 to $250,000. A gambler's livelihood. You might hit the jackpot, but most times you'll barely scrape by. I can't see the attraction. I'm not saying I wouldn't like to strike it rich, only with the stakes so high, you'd never be satisfied. This stone might be worth a bit, though.

There is a Lansdowne Corporation Land Cruiser outside the largest portacabin. I cut across the machine tracks and knock on the door. One of the foreman is sitting on a table beside a mega fan, reading what looks like a porn magazine. The room is bare, except for a box of files, a table lamp, and a thin mattress and blanket, which this man probably slept on last night.

'I'm looking for Edward Harvey,' I say.

'You and the rest of us. You won't find him here. Take one of these.' Before I can respond, he thrusts a piece of paper at me and an envelope. 'Fill it in and send it back to us. We'll look after the rest. Is there anyone else, do you know? My contract's up today. I can leave a few of these with you, if you like.'

I study the front page – a compensation claim form for the miners. Housing rights. 'I'm Edward's brother,' I tell him.

The foreman tugs at his thick beard, cracks his knuckles, and looks inanely at whatever is just above my head. 'Sorry, mate, I didn't realise.'

'You're encouraging people to sue, is that it?'

'It's company policy to look after the workers. Not up to me. I'm just following orders.' He offers me a Lucky Strike. When I refuse, he lights one for himself.

'Does Edward know? Have any of you bothered to tell him?'

'I'm just handing out the forms. It was *your* daughter who went missing, wasn't it?'

I nod, hoping he will have the sense to stop.

'Got two of my own. Sent them back home when Billy Walker's woman disappeared. Most of 'em with children left around then. No point in taking chances.' He draws on his cigarette and watches the smoke curl up in the draught from the fan. He's not the first person to talk to me as if I'm some kind of idiot. Only an idiot would let his daughters loose in Akarula. Unable to find a parting word, I leave.

Once I reach the main track, I start to run. I should have taken one of those forms to show Eddie. At least he could prepare himself, find some kind of defence, flee the country. I don't know. I wouldn't like to be in his shoes. (Never thought I'd hear myself say that.) It's only when I stop to catch my breath that it dawns on me – Eddie isn't here. He's not in the street. I checked the whole way round the service station. I'd have seen him if he was walking through the scrub – you can't hide. And now I've checked the mine. The truck is undrivable – Caroline has seen to that. A pain shoots right down my neck, lodging itself in my gut, the same pain I've had this past month. What if he's gone too? I picture myself ringing Delaney from Eddie's office. I play the conversation in my head, then there's the search, the waiting … and then … do we go to Adelaide, or do we stay here because we all know that people don't just disappear? Adrenalin fires through me; I'm getting ready to run for my life, only there's nothing to run away from except my own damn fear.

I barely notice the track or how far I've gone. I keep moving until I see the water tank – a large steel belly on legs. That's where he is. He's fixing the water. There was no one left for him to send out. And he had to walk because of the state of the truck. See how easy it is to get carried away, to let your imagination take over? My shoulders slacken slightly but the clicking sound in my ears gets louder.

A narrow path veers left towards the tank. It's not a path so much as a trampled-down section of scrub grass. In any case, I shout, 'Eddie!' There is no response, but if he's round the back, he might not hear. Sound gets swallowed up in all this open space, or else it carries for miles. Probably something to do with the temperature.

When I get nearer the tank, I notice that the ground is wet. A small pool of water sits on the impervious surface. The tank plug is loose; a continual thin stream of water leaks out. Someone must have unscrewed the plug. I find a good-sized stone and bang on the side of the tank, which rings hollow. At least the pump still works. I screw the plug back in.

'Eddie!' I walk right round. Who would have deliberately sabotaged the water system? I step back to take a look at the top of the tank and find that the ceiling cap is off.

I start to climb the ladder. The iron rungs are red hot. At the top, I try dragging the cap back on. It's heavy and scorches my hands. I have to haul myself up to the top rung to get more leverage. I peer down to see how much water is left inside. It's so black in there; I can't see a thing, only white lights bouncing off the surface. It takes a while for my eyes to adjust. Gradually the specks of white light disappear and I can see a shape, a body, a man's body. Eddie is curled up like a baby on the bottom of the tank.

I freeze. Can't think. I hang onto the edge of the opening to stop myself from falling in. My hands burn, my hat slips off and drops down into the water. An inch or two of water, not enough to drown a man. Not enough… Eddie? What's going on? What are you doing down there? 'Eddie!' His name bounces back at me. A searing pain in my gut. I forget to breathe. What have you done? And then I roar, as loud as I can, to wake him up, to make him look at me: 'Eddie!' In the silence that follows, a horsefly lands on my arm and bites.

Eddie couldn't swim, never learnt. Water terrified him. I stare down that hole until my mind goes blank. My brother's shape appears and disappears as the sun slips in and out of the morning sky. And I am suddenly cut free. The air seems to dance around me.

I climb down the ladder with no sense of how far I've gone or when I will reach the bottom. The rungs don't burn anymore; I have no sensation left in my fingers. When I finally stand on the ground, it feels hollow. Clouds multiply, and a wedge-tailed eagle makes that hawking guttural cry.

Why? Why?

After a while, I lose all sense of myself, feeling light and let go of. We didn't talk about Father. If we'd have talked… It was Eddie who found him, the year of the big snow. We'd gone to visit after Mother phoned. She said: 'Your father's gone.' No explanation. Father was slumped on a deckchair in the greenhouse, which was empty, being winter, and spotless. Every seed tray wiped clean. I didn't notice the blood and the cuts so much as his moustache: frozen solid. There was a bottle of gin knocked over at his feet. The autopsy said he had large amounts of medication in his system and had probably contracted hypothermia. When the police emptied his jacket pockets later on, they found a queen of hearts playing card folded over. On the back was scribbled 'Please forgive me, Margaret. Give my love to the boys.' Eddie and I made our final pact that day, not to talk about it to anyone, not even to each other. As far as I know, Eddie kept his word.

Retracing my footsteps back through the scrub to the main track, I sense God, not some religious God, but that tidal force that moves through us, destroying and creating simultaneously. I feel it, almost see it – a blade of grass cutting through stone – overwhelming and impossible. Why did he unscrew the plug, just enough so he had time to drown? To let us know? Was this

his way of saying goodbye? Did he know that I would find him?

When I get to the street, the bald man's car has gone and so have the last two houses. It's like a pseudo town, phantom houses with invisible walls. Was it because he couldn't bear to lose his town? When we were young he had this dream, this belief that anything was possible. We both did, for a while, like all kids. But then Eddie went ahead alone. He did it; he made the dream. A boy with a balloon who kept hanging on, rising higher and higher, never thinking of what might happen when the balloon finally bursts.

I arrive at the service station and walk between the pumps. Caroline waves a spade in the air, calling me over: 'We've been waiting for you. Where've you been?' She's kneeling on the ground at the foot of Red Rock Mountain, a few yards from the caravan. Moni is knelt down beside her. In a flash it dawns on me that someone could have done that to Eddie. Someone could have murdered him.

'Just a minute,' I shout, running for the shop. With my back pressed up against the door, I face the shelves of food and car supplies, almost deafened by the pounding of my own heart beat. What now? I can see him so clearly, curled up on the bottom of that tank. Of course Eddie wasn't murdered. Suicide makes too much sense.

I call Susan. The buttons on the office phone are stiff; it takes two attempts before I get through. She recognises my voice immediately. 'Mr Markarrwala's condition has stabilised in the last hour. All the signs are good. You got back ok?'

I make some kind of croaking sound as I try to speak.

'Is Monica alright? Did they find…?'

'It's Eddie.' I can hear her holding her breath, but I don't know how to continue. And then the door opens and Caroline is standing there. Seeing her somehow releases me; I just say it. 'I found him in the water tank.'

Whatever Susan says in reply gets washed up in Caroline's face, leaving a wreckage of disbelieving lines. Caroline gravitates towards me without seeming to move, and takes the phone from my hand. She tells Susan we will contact her as soon as we reach Adelaide. The receiver gets dropped and bangs against the cupboard; there is a constant drone. Caroline holds onto me. We stay caught up in each other for a long time. I don't have the strength to push her away.

Caroline takes my hands, turning them palm up. They're covered in blisters – a few have burst.

'It's not as bad as it looks,' I tell her. 'Did he say anything to you?'

She shakes her head, guiding me through to the bathroom, and dresses my hands with antiseptic bandages.

'Where's Moni?' I ask, as she secures the pins.

'I told her to wait in the caravan. We should go.'

She doesn't seem shocked or sad, just empty.

'We'll tell her later,' I say, unable to face the idea right now.

We head across the tarmac.

Moni spots us through the window. 'We're going to bury the bird,' she says, jumping up from the table and racing out to meet us. 'What's wrong with your hands?'

'I burnt them,' I say.

She leads me around the caravan to the spot where she was kneeling earlier on. There is a mound of earth and small stones. 'Mum said you'd say a prayer.'

Caroline and I crouch on either side of Moni as she says: 'Do you think she'll be able to fly when she wakes up? If I was a bird, I'd just fly straight to heaven. I wouldn't wait until I died.'

I study the small grave, trying to find a response. 'I used to think heaven didn't exist, for anyone. Now I'm not so sure. Who's to say there isn't somewhere for birds to go to when they die.' I draw Moni towards me. 'Nothing is impossible, when you think about it.'

'Will you say the prayer now?' she asks, drawing back from me in anticipation.

'A prayer. Right. Close your eyes.' As Moni closes her eyes, I look across at Caroline. The muscles in her face falter as she tries not to cry.

'For the bird that got shot down, we pray that it may find its way to heaven or the place where birds go to when they stop breathing.'

'How will it find its way?' Moni asks, her eyes now wide with concern.

'Birds are clever creatures. Remember the swallows, all the way from Africa. They always found our shed, didn't they?'

'But Georgie's not a swallow.'

'Heaven will find her.'

Moni's face lights up for a second. 'We should make a cross.'

She starts poking around the tyres and sparse scrub at the back of the caravan, looking for sticks. I search with her. Neither of us notices Caroline leaving. Moni chooses two sticks from the pile we collect. I do the best I can, tying the sticks together with a piece of scrub grass – not an easy feat with bandaged hands. We lay the cross on the mound; the earth is too dry to hold it upright.

'That's fine,' Moni says, tugging my shirt sleeve as we head back across the tarmac.

Later, when Moni is in bed, I phone the police, who tell me to leave Eddie where he is until the morning. And then I call Susan again. After that, I sort through Eddie's things. The piles of paper are easily packed. It's the plans, his precious plans for Akarula that I don't know what to do with. I peel them off the wall. Every building is mapped out in minute detail. A railway line, for goodness sake. The whole idea was ridiculous, impossible, yet somehow he managed to pull off … if not most of it, the important part. He made a town. Which is a damn sight more than I can boast about.

Caroline raps on the window. The outside light gives her a ghostly appearance. She's holding one of the boxes that were stacked behind the shed ready for moving. If the rain comes before we're finished, they'll be ruined.

When I open the window, she thrusts the box towards me. 'Take it,' she says, wearing a determined expression that hides everything else.

Then she passes me another one.

'Is Moni asleep?' she asks.

'Think so.'

The last box gets stuck at an awkward angle and is now rammed in too far to be pushed back. Caroline tugs from her side, and I pull from mine. Eventually the box breaks. I don't know what to do with my half.

'Give it to me,' she says, reaching through the window. But I don't give it to her. I clamp the rotten dusty scrap of cardboard to my chest. Whatever she is standing on – most likely a beer crate – makes her able to lean right in, while she holds onto the frame for support. 'Give it to me,' she repeats. She is half-in, half-out of the window. Her fingers grip the ledge. I study the tiny flecks of varnish clinging to her nails without attempting a reply, but she's insistent. 'Michael, for God's sake, we're going to have to talk about it some time.'

'Talk about what?'

'You're right.' She stops, and when she starts again, her voice is softer. 'If it will make things easier, I can stay. At least I won't be in your way. Moni doesn't want me either; I know she doesn't. And now Eddie.'

'What about Eddie?'

'Do you think it's my fault?'

I pause, trying to register what she means, and then say: 'What you do is up to you.'

The remains of the box slip through my hands. I turn away from the window and go back to the desk. Each drawer contains another pile of notices. My eyes catch words and phrases, but not enough to make sense: red statements at the bottom of a page. Eddie is home and dry. We're the ones left picking up the pieces. Yet again, he has walked away scot-free. Caroline has gone when I look back. A stream of insects flies in through the open window. England has never felt so far away.

Eddie's filing cabinet is stuffed with notebooks full of sketches, two-line ideas, doodles; where is the evidence of a businessman? He wasn't the wheeler-dealer people thought him; just played the role, wore the cap – managed to convince everyone because he had convinced himself. He wanted to be the Prime Minister at one stage. Maybe he would have made a better job of that, surrounded by advisors; he had no one to advise him, no one to rein in his wild fantasies and lay out the actual facts.

High-pitched voices start up in the sitting room. When I open the door, I find Moni and Caroline flinging words at each other like snowballs packed tight to give a punch. Both of them spin round when they see me.

Caroline gets in first. 'She did it again. Tell her she can't do that.'

'Do what?' It's not unusual for me to act as umpire. Two headstrong women – well, Moni is still a girl, but sometimes, when she flashes that temper, I can see clearly the woman she will become. She has fallen silent, staring into me with her glistening eyes: the picture of sadness in her orange cardigan. She sleeps in that cardigan now.

Caroline is sharp on the defence. 'Talking as if Georgie is in the room. What is she trying to do? Torture us all?' She swivels back round to Moni. 'Do you think it's funny?'

Moni settles her gaze on the wooden floor.

'It's just too hard when you do that,' Caroline says, relenting a little. 'Can you try not to do it? Please try.'

I step between them. 'Your mum's tired. We're all tired. Why don't you get back into bed? We've got a busy day tomorrow.' I help her onto the camp bed and kiss her cheek, pushing her hair back off her face. She has no idea how precious she is.

I draw Caroline into the office and close the door. 'Why did you shout at her?'

Caroline stays resolute, her arms folded across her chest. 'It's Georgie's voice. She uses Georgie's voice. How does she do that?'

There are tears in her eyes as I lead her on into Eddie's bedroom. 'Get some sleep.' I say, pulling back the cover and adjusting the pillow. I leave her in the quarter-moon-darkness to get undressed.

Later, I find her curled up on Eddie's bed, still dressed, her haunting green eyes staring out. Wheeling the chair in from Eddie's office, I sit in the corner of the bedroom and wait until she falls asleep.

The last place to sort through is Eddie's shed. I take the key from the hook in the hall, go outside and unlock the padlock. With a torch, I assess the size of the task ahead of me. This doesn't look like Eddie's shed. As with his office, all the shelves have been tidied: nails in the nail box, tools hanging on the wall in their rightful places. Only a large cardboard box with a plastic bag taped to the top obstructs the floor. I try to push the box over to the wall but it weighs a ton. Taking a Stanley knife from the tool box, I make a hole, then cut one side of the box away. It's a projector, a full-sized cinema projector. Once I cut through the plastic bag on top, I find a reel of tape, and a square paper note: Happy Birthday, Mike.

I push the projector outside and point the lens at the back wall of Eddie's house, before running an electric cable through the office window. It takes me a while to figure out how to work the thing and where to put the reel. When I flick the switch, the reel starts turning and a square of light hits the wall, a mass of grey flecks. I sit on the tarmac and wait for the picture to start.

And there I am, aged twelve, running around in that fringed cowboy suit, firing a gun. The camera bounces as Eddie runs after me. In my head, I can hear us shouting at each other.

'You can't shoot and be the sheriff at the same time.' That's me.

'I'm Castro,' Eddie says.

Eddie was always Castro and I was always Egor. We both had magical powers and could do just about anything. Egor, the fearless. And I *was* fearless, and brave. As I watch myself leap over what must have been the rabbit hutch in our parents' garden, something rips inside me and all the things I've packed away over the years tumble out. I can't stop them. My tears make the film look smudged.

I must have taken hold of the camera because Eddie is running now; he keeps looking back and waving. 'Come on, Mike. Look out Father, Egor's coming!' Father is sitting in a wooden deckchair, cleaning his boots. He throws his hands in the air as Eddie points the gun. 'Alright, boys, what do you want? Don't shoot.' He did a pretty good job, our father, when I think about it.

The reel tugs as it reaches the end, but I carry on with that day, going down to the river with Eddie to catch fish in plastic bags. Eddie almost falls in and I laugh at his panic and do a stupid dance, snagging my leg on a bramble, which makes Eddie laugh. We find a rotting sheep and get a stick and poke around inside. I think we make a fire too, but that could have been another day. We were the same back then, Eddie and I.

I replay the film over and over.

'The police have arrived.' Caroline's voice sounds as if it's coming from a distance. 'I heard a plane about ten minutes ago.' As I shake off the remains of sleep, I slowly realise that I'm in the shed, and pull myself up with the help of the projector. It's light again. The sky is a mess of thick clouds.

Caroline doesn't ask why I've slept in the shed. She glances at the projector and then says: 'Moni's waiting for you. I've made coffee.' She looks like a worn-out copy of herself.

Moni is sitting crossed-legged on Eddie's bed when I go in. I sit down beside her.

Caroline talks to us from Eddie's office. 'Maybe we can make a fire later? Cook some food outside. What do you think?'

Moni looks at me warily – she doesn't trust this talk.

'What do you think, Moni?' I ask.

She loves fires. We used to take her to the sea, to Caroline's parents, on her birthday, build a fire on the beach, have a picnic, before Georgie was born.

'Can we?'

I wink and she winks back.

As I head out, she asks 'Where are you going?'

I glance at Caroline, who narrows her eyes and mouths for me to say something. So I do. 'Uncle Eddie had an accident yesterday.'

'Is he dead?'

I nod, unable to find more of an explanation.

Moni doesn't blink. It's as if she can't quite take it in, and then she says to Caroline, 'Shall we play Scrabble?'

Detective Delaney and Walsh are accompanied by two other men: a sandy-haired fellow with rough features and a navy sports cap, and a younger chap who gesticulates wildly as he talks. As I reach the bend, I stop to watch them tramp across the scrub at the edge of the airstrip. Walsh waves. The sight of them sends my head spinning.

We walk as far as the tree. The youngest one moves in under the branches and we all follow. A silence cuts through the tail end of our greeting. It's as if we've broken into someone's home and the alarm has gone off. Delaney says we'd better move on.

When we have veered off onto the mine road and made some distance, Walsh asks, 'What happened?' eyeing my bandages.

I throw my hands into the air and lift my chin slightly by way of answering. And then, perhaps because we are almost there, I dive in, dredging up the details, plucking out the key points. 'Eddie couldn't swim. He was always terrified of water.' I've said all this before, on the phone last night, but not like this. Once I start, I'm like a burst pipe; everything floods out: bits and pieces about Father and how Eddie always overstepped the mark.

'Georgie was a lot like Eddie,' I say, realising this only now.

I hardly notice the two men from forensics head on towards the tank. I continue talking, thinking, tripping over myself in my rush to get to the end. Then I notice the pile of equipment in front of the water tank. They must have thrown it out of the plane on their way.

'You needn't watch this,' Walsh says, as we stop within yards of the sight. But I carry on, showing Delaney how the plug was out and how the lid was off.

'We'll do the rest,' she says, signalling for Walsh to get rid of me. She doesn't want me to see the body. 'Let us know when you get to Adelaide. We can talk you through the procedure then. We'll need to do an autopsy. You might want to make arrangements for a funeral.'

I can hear them unzipping a bag on the other side of the tank. They are going to put my brother in a zip-up bag.

'How's Monica?' Walsh asks, as he directs me back along the mine road. 'At least the rain's on its way.' The sky visibly blackens as he speaks.

I stop to let him know that I can go on alone.

Walsh scratches the back of his hand. 'We'll call in to say goodbye,' he offers, before turning back.

Eddie's water-tight body bobs to the surface of my mind as I drift along towards the service station. I try to picture his face, the lines around his eyes, his sharp chin, but all I see is Father's white frosted moustache. And a pair of hands.

The removal van has taken most of our belongings to Susan's house. I sent the projector; we can always sell it. There's a refreshing emptiness to the caravan and most of Eddie's rooms. I pile the rest of his clothes and papers in a heap on the tarmac, ready for burning. I put the film reel there too. I'll never watch it again.

At dusk, Moni and I collect wood for the fire and poke it underneath Eddie's things, shifting the more flammable items to the bottom. Caroline is preparing a meal with the remains in the fridge.

'Do you think Georgie will be able to see our fire, if we build it big enough?' Moni throws a bundle of sticks on top of Eddie's clothes.

'Maybe. That depends on where she is.'

'She's in the sea.'

'Why would she be in the sea?'

Moni stops what she is doing and looks at me. 'Mrs. Thompson in Hendon School told us that some people believe that when you die you turn into the thing you most want to be. Is that true?'

'Well, I can't say it isn't true because I don't know. We believe whatever fits into the way we think, but that doesn't mean everything else is wrong, and it doesn't mean that what we believe in is right. You can't believe everything you're told.'

'Do you remember how Mrs Thompson lost her hair and had to wear that turban? I bet she'd be a dog. She loves dogs. Or maybe an apple.' Moni picks some sleep from her eye. 'What will you turn into when you die?' Moni asks.

I take my time thinking of the right reply. 'That's a hard one. Let me see. I think I'll be that matchbox you keep in your pocket, so I can keep my eye on you.'

Moni laughs – it's the most beautiful sound.

I poke in the last of the wood, thinking about Moni's old teacher, who somehow managed to survive, despite the odds. Moni asks. 'I'm going to be a bird,' Moni says. 'An eagle or a kingfisher. I don't mind which.'

We position three crates to sit on. Moni hasn't mentioned Eddie. Sometimes with children, if you're lucky, these things can wash right through without a trace of sadness.

I light the fire while we wait for Caroline. With a splash of petrol, the flames swell, forming a tower of smoke. We sit watching the sky, seeing if we can spot the moment when the day slips into night.

Caroline arrives with kangaroo steaks and a good chunk of bread.

'This is the lot,' she says. 'I've thrown the rest away. Eddie had the whole carcass in the freezer.'

Moni refuses to eat kangaroo, and tucks into a slice of buttered bread instead.

Caroline slaps a steak onto my plate and hands me a knife and a fork. She's wearing an opal bracelet I haven't seen before; some present from Eddie, no doubt. He bought us all presents. Spoilt the girls rotten. His catch phrase was 'It's only money.' I suppose he was right about that.

I pour some wine into the plastic caravan mugs we are going to leave behind. We listen to the fire spit and crackle, and talk nonsense for a while. Absorbed in the flames and this feast, I forget for a moment where I am.

Moni puts her plate down on the ground and says, 'I can see a castle and a dragon and a tree.'

It's a game we used to play, watching the fire, seeing what we could see.

'I can see a pumpkin, a yawning mouth, and a dog's head,' Caroline says, looking at me.

'I can see a family dancing, wings, broken waves on the sea.'

We keep on staring into the fire, saying what we can see, until Moni gets tired.

'Are we really leaving tomorrow?' she asks, as she follows Caroline into the caravan.

'The plane is picking us up in the morning.' I blow her a kiss.

Caroline sings Moni a bedtime song. I haven't heard this one before.

Half a hundred days passed away
and still no footprints I can recognise
tracing shores we walked
familiar rocks seem strange
and the land is torched
with someone else's light.

There is no way I can look to tomorrow
No way I can say
That a new dawn
Will be washing the old one away.

The song goes on, but I stop listening to the words, concentrating on the notes instead, feeling myself rise and fall with each rainbow of sound. When Caroline comes back out, she stands behind me. 'Could you really see a family?' she asks.

'Did you see a pumpkin?'

She pulls her crate up close to mine and hunches down, holding on to her ankles. 'Is this it?' Her voice dies away as she stares into the fire, now half the size it was. 'Dad always said I didn't deserve you.'

'Your father…' There is so much I could say about Caroline's father.

After a while I ask: 'Did you love Eddie?' I want the truth, even though, at this stage, I don't think I really care.

'Yes,' she says, without hesitation. 'Like a fool. It's true what they say about not knowing what you've got until it's gone.'

The way she looks at me, it's hard to tell whether she is talking about Eddie or me.

She goes back into the caravan, returning with two boxes, and puts one down at my feet: Georgie's clothes, a few toys, rolls of paper.

'Don't you want to keep any of this?' I ask, flicking through the pictures: scribbles of colour.

Caroline flings the box onto the fire. She loses her balance as she lets go, falling in after it. Her hair catches fire. I drag her out and douse her head with a wet tea-towel to stop the flames. The smell of her burnt hair is repugnant.

'What the hell are you doing?' I kick the other box into the fire, out of rage. Her beautiful auburn hair is scorched on one side.

'It doesn't hurt,' she says, dusting off the crate before she sits.

A silent hour passes as we watch the fire burn down to smoking embers. I think back to what she's said, roll the words over in my mind. Did she mean Eddie or me?

'Will you cut my hair?' she asks, jumping up.

'With these?' I hold up my bandaged hands.

'It doesn't matter what it looks like.'

She fetches a pair of scissors from the caravan. Handing them over, she shifts her crate in front of mine and sits with her back to me. I snip off the ends first, managing to make a hacking motion with the scissors, afraid to do too much, and then gradually I start to make deeper cuts – I actually enjoy it – until she is left with a short back and sides. She looks so different; her face has hollowed out. But in an odd way, despite the roughness of the cut, it actually suits her.

She runs her hands over her head and says, 'I'm going to bed.' Before she goes, she throws her crate onto the fire and collects the plates, retreating with them into the caravan. I listen to her washing up. Eventually she turns the light out, and I am left with the dying fire. Thunder rumbles in the distance. It's pitch dark. Every sound is amplified. This is what I imagine it would be like in a submarine, this echoing circular silence. The night air holds its breath, waiting to burst. I wish I knew how long Georgie had been in that shaft before … before what? When I close my eyes, I can see her on the road. Perhaps that was her way of saying goodbye? The longer I stay in Akarula, the more open to the world's mysteries I become, because nothing makes sense when you think about it.

Moni wakes me up.

'Mum cut her hair. She looks like Mrs Thompson. Come on, we have to say goodbye before the plane arrives.' She drags me out of bed and stamps around outside impatiently while I get dressed.

'Goodbye to whom?' Doesn't she realise that we are the only ones left?

'Come on!'

'Are you not coming?' I ask Caroline, who is scrubbing the table. Her haircut looks coarser in the daylight.

'I want to finish off.' She flits from one side of the table to the other, her eyes darting. Finish off? We haven't talked about what will happen when we get to Adelaide. I've rented a one-bedroom flat.

'Don't be long. Please.'

She starts hauling the cushions off the benches and wiping the plywood tops underneath. It's her way of saying goodbye to a place.

When I step outside, the air is pulsing; there is a layer of swelling cloud, which makes the light syrupy. Moni insists on climbing Red Rock Mountain.

'We'll see better from the top,' she says as we start the ascent, scanning the crevices and clumps of scrub grass for snakes.

She scrambles on ahead, turning round now and then to check I'm still behind her. The rock gets steeper near the top. I have difficulty hauling myself up. My hands feel raw; the bandages give no protection. In this light, the earth seems redder, lending a sharpness to the landscape; everything has a clear edge.

Moni is sitting on one of the flat rocks when I finally make it to the top. It takes me a while to get my breath back. There is quite a view. The bush stretches out as far as the horizon. You look differently when you're looking at something for the last time. You look for the imprint, the soul behind the shape, the lines and marks that will help you to remember.

Moni plonks herself down beside me, pressing her body up against mine. 'I know what happens to these,' she says, holding the shell of a cicada between her finger and thumb, pointing through the lattice framework of skin. 'You were right. It must be strange, getting a whole new skin. How often do snakes shed their skins?'

'Once, twice a year. I'm not sure. We'll have to look it up. Might be different for each species.'

She lays the cicada skin down where she is sitting and slips off to do some rock-hunting, leaving me to contemplate Akarula. The branches of the ghost gum tree seem to move to a rhythm of their own. I must visit Mr M in the hospital once we're settled.

Moni bobs up from behind one of the rocks and scribbles something in her notebook. She pulls out a reddish-brown ground beetle from her pocket and makes a sketch, measuring it with her index finger before she lets it go.

'I've got something for you,' I say, waving her over. I show her the opal I found. 'We can get it made into a necklace if you like, or a small hat.'

She grins, rolling it between her palms before dropping it into her pocket. 'Thanks,' she says. And then she mumbles something about Uncle Eddie and the colour of the sea, making it clear that I don't need to understand.

We say goodbye: goodbye mine, goodbye street, goodbye birds, goodbye caravan. There are silent goodbyes for everything else. Moni takes a sip of water from her bottle before offering some to me.

'Do you think Uncle Eddie and Georgie are in the same place?' she asks.

'They might be.'

'Why did he drown?'

I've already thought of an answer, but when I start, this comes out instead. 'Occasionally people decide to give up. He was a big dreamer, your uncle. When dreams get too big, they can swallow you. They can trick you into doing all sorts of things.'

'Was he very sad?'

'I think so. Do you know what you need to do when you're sad – to stop the sadness growing?' Moni shakes her head. 'Hold a happy thought inside your mind, something that makes you smile, something really good. When you start to feel sad, you get it out and think about it, make it as big as you can.'

'I know what my happy thought is.'

I wait for her to tell me, but she doesn't. Whatever she is thinking plays around her eyes, making them sparkle.

We stand on the summit, staying absolutely still for a moment. That's when the snake appears, a brown one, sliding over a rock not two yards in front of us, flicking out its tongue, hesitating, giving us time to get a good look before it slithers back into the undergrowth. Together we let out a celebratory howl.

'Do you think it was poisonous?' Moni asks, breathless with excitement.

'Probably.'

'I think it was.'

She races down the rocky face to tell her mother. I follow her, taking my time, not really wanting to reach the bottom.

The plane arrives just as I get to the caravan. Caroline is standing in front of the steps, her string bag draped over her shoulder, her sunhat shading the best part of her face. She is holding Georgie's clogs. Moni leaps around her in circles.

As I go into the caravan, Caroline says: 'I've checked the cupboards.'

There is not a scrap of evidence to suggest that anyone lived here. I close the curtains and pick up the suitcases, trundling them down the steps. Seeing me struggle, Caroline puts the clogs into her bag and takes one of the cases from me. 'I can manage,' she says. The three of us walk in procession up the road to the bend and head out across the scrub towards the airstrip.

'I'd like to be a pilot,' Moni says, skipping up beside me. She waves at Denis, a tall burly type who is standing in a cloud of dust. He comes over to greet us.

'Maybe Denis can show you a few things.'

Denis takes the suitcase from Caroline and leads Moni up the plane steps. I'm on the steps myself when Caroline lets out a sob behind me. I turn to see her standing on the dirt track, her mouth fixed in a determined half-smile. She signals for me to go on. What is she doing? She can't stay out here on her own? From the plane, I watch her take Georgie's clogs out of her bag and carefully lay them on the ground. Denis calls for her to get a move on. He doesn't know what she is doing.

She nods at him, walking around the clogs towards the plane with that half-smile anchored to her face. And then she makes her way up the steps and comes to sit down next to me, fastening her seatbelt like she did the day we went on the big wheel, our first real date, wearing the same shrunken expression. While Denis pulls up the steps, she takes off her hat, smoothing down what is left of her hair. Her lips are quivering.

As we take off, both of us watch Georgie's clogs disappear into a cloud of dust. Moni, sitting up front in the cockpit, next to Denis, turns around to us and grins. I do a thumbs-up at her.

'Heard about the abo getting hurt,' Denis yells back as he makes a turn over the service station. 'Nasty business. You'd think folk would learn. Did they ever find the bodies?'

He doesn't know it was our child. All those times he flew us to Wattle Creek, I kept my mouth shut. It was always a relief to meet someone who didn't know. We curve upwards, away from the street. Denis starts explaining the buttons and levers to Moni, shouting over the engine noise.

Caroline cries silently. I imagine taking hold of her hand, how it would feel.

Denis says, 'We're due some rain. You want to see this place when it rains.'

I close my eyes and picture Akarula filling up with water.

MONICA

After five days in Adelaide, we find this house. There's a swing fixed to a big tree in the back garden. It's much better than the flat we were staying in, which only had one bedroom, and no bath. People talked outside the window in the middle of the night and woke us up. Me and Mum slept in the double bed and Dad stayed on the settee. The whole place smelt of rubber bands. I found chewing gum wedged underneath the table. We were glad to leave.

I wish we could go back to England. I asked if we could go home, but Mum said we couldn't leave Georgie in Australia on her own. She doesn't understand that Georgie isn't alive; she's not dead either. I can hear her, but I can't see her. It must be strange, being invisible. Mr M would know all about that.

Dad asks me if I want to go with him to Wattle Creek to collect our things from the doctor's house. There's nothing to do in Adelaide – until Monday, when I start school (it's my birthday on Monday too) – so I tell Dad I'll go. I want to see Mr M, anyway. Did you know Uncle Eddie killed himself?

We get up before the sun. Mum makes me drink some orange juice, and brews a flask of coffee for Dad. Her hair looks better since she went to the hairdressers.

'Drink plenty of water,' she tells me. 'Have you got Mr M's present?'

I bought him a wooden egg – it's the size of a normal egg, only wooden. I've wrapped it in purple tissue paper. It's in my rucksack, which Mum has; she's packing sandwiches and drinks for our journey.

'When do you think you'll be back?' she asks Dad.

'Thursday. Friday if we get delayed. I'd rather not drive at night.'

While Dad is putting on his coat, Mum smokes a cigarette out of the kitchen window, tapping her ash into a saucer. I check through my rucksack to see if she's forgotten anything. When I say goodbye, she squeezes me, kissing the top of my head. She won't let go. I have to push her off. She tells me to say hello to Mr M, and her eyes go all watery.

We get into the van.

'You ready, champ?' Dad says, starting the engine. As we drive off, I wave at Mum, who is standing by the gate. Dad keeps his eyes on the road.

Wattle Creek is miles away. We sing for a while, but Dad can't sing like Mum, so we turn the radio on. We pass through lots of small towns that get smaller the farther away from Adelaide we get. And the air heats up all the time. After hours of driving, we are back on a red chalky road. A herd of long-legged emus run out in front of us. Dad stops the van so we can get a look. They go so fast I don't get chance to take a picture. (Dad's given me one of Uncle Eddie's old cameras.)

We can't stop for long because it's too hot. When we start moving again, I stick my head out of the window and feel the wind beat against my face like a giant fan. Flies hit the windscreen; every now and then Dad leans out of the van to wipe them off. There are dark spots in the blue sky, which are probably wedge-tailed eagles. You can't really see them.

We drive all day. I count the termite mounds, which would look like witches hats if they were black.

'We're not far now,' Dad says, as we join a tarmac road. My bum hurts from sitting, and I've got a pain in my neck from resting my head against the seatbelt. I watch the sky turn into raspberry ripple ice-cream as the sun fades away. There are lots of clouds.

At the outskirts of Wattle Creek it starts to rain, small drops at first, and then it hammers down. Dad drives through the town with his wipers on top speed. When we reach the doctor's house, which is in a street of houses a bit like Akarula, I stand by the van, tilt my head back with my eyes closed and try to catch the rain in my mouth. Dad tells me to go inside – the doctor, Susan, has the door open – but instead I run up and down the street with my arms stretched out like a B52 bomber plane, firing at everything. The rain feels stone-heavy as it splashes down on me. Dad and Susan are laughing in the doorway, and then Dad grabs Susan's hand and pulls her out onto the street. The three of us jump in all the puddles and get soaking wet.

'Call the coastguard!' Dad shouts over the rain. It's a line from a film.

'Send him in, Jack,' I shout back. A black and white film me and Dad watched years ago.

Susan says: 'Come in before you drown.' She's the first to go inside.

After I've dried off and put my spare clothes on, we have dinner: some kind of meat stew with boiled potatoes. Dad and Susan talk as if they've forgotten that I'm sitting at the table.

'I read your article,' Susan says, pouring Dad more wine. 'I liked the fact that you contacted the other families.'

'I wanted to know how they were dealing with it.'

'I was surprised by Billy Walker.' (I don't know who Billy Walker is.) 'To admit in a national paper that he'd beaten his wife because she was pregnant with someone else's child – that's pretty brave. Did he tell you who he thought the father was?'

'Nope.'

She fills her own wine glass.

I take another potato to soak up the last bit of stew. Dad and Susan have stopped eating. They're both holding their wine-glasses up; the backs of their hands almost touch.

'Do you miss him?' she says to Dad. Her lips have gone purple in the middle from the wine.

Dad doesn't answer. For a second their fingers touch.

'What are you doing?' I push my plate away.

'Putting you to bed,' Dad says. He sets his glass on the table and pulls out my chair.

'Will you come too?' I ask him.

'In a bit.'

I say goodnight to Susan and then Dad takes me through the hall to our bedroom, which is full of things we brought from England.

I open one of the flaps on the box that is taking up most of the room. 'What's this?'

'Something Uncle Eddie gave me.'

It's funny Dad says that, because the giant camera inside sort of reminds me of Uncle Eddie. I have to climb over it to get into bed.

'Do you like Susan?' I say, when we've done all the stuff we normally do before lights out.

Dad nods. 'I think she's special. Do you?'

I give him a kiss goodnight and tell him to leave the door open.

The room is nearly empty when I wake up; all the big boxes have gone. I lie in bed listening to the sounds coming from the kitchen: hushed voices, cups or plates being put down. Dad creeps in for another box. When he notices that my eyes are open, he says, 'Come on, lazy bones. Mr M's waiting for us.'

I get dressed as quickly as I can. 'Are we driving back to Adelaide today?' I ask him, as we go into the kitchen.

'Tomorrow. Early morning.' Dad bites into a piece of buttered toast Susan has made him.

'You look nice,' I tell her, because she does. She is wearing a sun-brown buttoned up dress and small clip-on earrings.

After we've finished breakfast and tidied up, Susan waves us off. She says she'll see us later. Me and Dad drive over to the hospital in the yellow van. Everything looks so clean after the rain, as if someone's painted over the whole town in shiny nail polish.

The nurse with the ponytail remembers my name. 'Hello, Monica,' she says. 'How are you today?' She smiles at Dad. Her teeth are really white. 'Dr Marshall said you'd be coming. You're his first visitors.' Her ponytail bounces up the corridor in front of us. 'Let's hope he's awake,' she says, pushing open a set of double doors. It's not a room; it's another long corridor with beds down either side. I don't see Mr M at first. The nurse stops and talks to one of the doctors, who gives her a clipboard to carry. Some of the people in here look really sick.

Mr M is in the second to last bed on the left-hand side. He's propped up on a stack of pillows, wearing a pair of green hospital pyjamas that make him look a bit like Grandpa. He's a lot thinner than Grandpa though; you can see all the bones in his face.

'You've got visitors.' the nurse says to Mr M. She pulls the curtain around, winking at me. 'Bit of privacy.'

I jump onto Mr M's bed and hug him over the sheet, but he screws up his face as if it hurts, and the nurse tells me to get off.

'He's not quite ready for that yet. Go gently with him,' she says, straightening his sheet before she leaves.

'What's wrong with you?' I ask him.

'I knew you'd come,' he says.

Dad and Mr M say a few words while I look in his cupboard. It's empty. I wish I'd brought him some flowers. Some of the other patients have flowers. All he's got is a plastic cup of water. The drawer is empty too. Then I remember the present at the bottom of my rucksack. While I'm looking for it, I find the bag of sandwiches we forgot to eat. The cheese has gone slimy and smells a bit, but I slip them into Mr M's drawer anyway, in case he gets hungry.

'Here you go,' I say, putting the wrapped egg on the sheet near his hand. I have to help him open it. He holds the egg flat on his palm, then closes his fingers and flips his hand over. BAM – the egg disappears, just like magic. Dad laughs; he thinks it's a trick. The next moment, Mr M makes the egg appear again.

'How did you do that?' I ask him.

He just smiles.

Dad is nodding as if he knows. 'I'm going to get some coffee. Can I get you anything, Mr M?'

'No, mate. Thanks.' He says *thanks* really loudly. The man in the end bed with the tube up his nose turns his head and looks over, twisting his mouth as if he's trying to smile.

'That's Gordon,' Mr M says, waving over at the man. 'Got attacked by a wallaby. Punched his lights out.' He laughs; it's so funny the way he laughs, like he's hiccuping. He has to stop because it hurts. Dad pulls the curtain back as he goes. And I flick Mr M's bedside light on and off, to check it's working.

'Why did those men hurt you?' I leave the light on.

He rolls the egg around in his hand, bringing it up to his nose to smell it. 'Thawurr babarlthang,' he says, smoothing his thumb over the wavy wood-lines. Sometimes he says things I don't understand. 'I've got a story for you.'

I nod. 'Georgie thinks you're BLAST,' I tell him.

He smiles again. His teeth are broken and some are missing altogether – not like the nurse's teeth.

'Don't you worry about your sister,' he says. 'She's alright where she is. You'll be right too.'

'Is it about the Rainbow Snake?' I ask.

'You'd better see if you can borrow that chair from Gordon.'

I go over to the man with the nose tube. He's got two chairs at the side of his bed and no one is sitting on them. He reaches out his fat hand and I shake it. His skin feels squidgy, as if it's full of water. I let go really quickly. One of the nurses helps me drag the chair across to Mr M's bed, and I sit down. 'When will you go back to Akarula?'

'Sometime and never. As long as our tree still stands, we'll be welcome.' Mr M has told me lots of stories, mostly about the Rainbow Snake, who made the rivers, and Baiame, who did almost everything else. Baiame and the Rainbow Snake are sort of the same, only different. The one about the sea is my favourite. I think I told you that Red Rock Mountain is the place where the Rainbow Snake sleeps. Well another thing I didn't say is that whatever grows and moves on Red Rock Mountain is part of Rainbow Snake's dreams. I don't know if that's true, but it might be. Mr M believes the snake is real. He also believes that the tree he sits under in Akarula is not really a tree; it's a relative of his, like Grandpa, only older. I told him once that I wouldn't want to be a tree – too boring. We were sitting right underneath his tree when I said that. He laughed and told me to shush, in case his relative was listening. I said I was sorry to the tree. I think it heard me too.

'This story,' Mr M starts, 'was passed down from the tail of the sacred river to the mouth of the sea.' His eyes always glaze over when he's telling a story, as if they've spun backwards and are looking inside instead of out. 'It's about the bora you folks call Akarula. Back then, you see, there were no houses. Our people lived under the sun, finding food along the lines sung out by our ancestors.

'But one day we heard a rumbling that would normally have come from the sky, only it was the earth talking. We listened, lying with our ears flat to the ground, and while we lay there, many trucks arrived. When the trucks stopped, the rumbling stopped, and this was taken as a sign. These trucks were full of white fellas with picks and drills. They started making holes, digging up the earth and all its treasure. Our people made way for these new travellers, waiting to hear their stories and songs. In exchange for food, the travellers gave us small coloured paper, which we burned, but it didn't last like wood, and soon the fires went out. One by one we were marched into the trucks, with promise of more paper, and driven away.'

'Is this a sad story?'

Mr M's eyes turn outwards for a second. 'Only one man, a man named Mali Ku, survived the rumbling. He stayed to watch Rainbow Snake and guard the bora. You see, the rumbling had woken her, and she was hungry; starving in fact. Mali Ku knew Rainbow Snake wouldn't sleep again until she'd eaten. The first thing she came upon was a man, one of the hole-digging white fellas. She swallowed him up in one giant gulp.' Mr M gulps as if he is the Rainbow Snake. 'The man tasted bitter, the kind of bitterness that grows from being alone. Rainbow Snake very nearly spat him out, but, feeling tired, she slept again. It wasn't long before the constant rumbling woke her a second time. Finding that her stomach was only half-full, she went in search of more food. This time she tried a woman. The woman was sweeter than the man; still there was a sad sourness in her blood that lingered like bad breath in Rainbow Snake's mouth.

'Once more the great snake closed her eyes. And her eyes would have stayed closed if it hadn't been for the cries of a lost child. Following these cries, Rainbow Snake slithered across the bush until she found a small girl in one of the white fella's holes, and so she swallowed her too, in the hope that the rumbling would finally stop and she would be left in peace. Do you know what the girl tasted like?' I shake my head. 'Honey. Mali Ku watched all this in silence, knowing what he must do. When night fell and Rainbow Snake grew still, Mali Ku took a big knife and slit open the side of her belly while she slept. Blood poured out, turning the rocks and all the land dark red. The pain woke her up, and she opened one eye. When she saw Mali Ku standing there with the bloodied knife, she knew what had happened and hissed with rage. But the three lost ones had already pushed their way out of the hole made by the knife, and escaped into the bush. Only now they looked different. The half-digested magic of Rainbow Snake's stomach had changed them into kangaroos. The lost ones went in search of their families, but their own people didn't recognise them.'

'It is a sad story. Does Mali Ku kill the Rainbow Snake in the end?'

'At first Rainbow Snake was so angry with Mali Ku that she laid curses on his head, making the white fellas beat him. In her rage, she commanded the sky to wash away her enemies. The rain fell hard and long. Rainbow Snake cleaned her wounds in the empty bora and drank the rivers dry.' Mr M stops for a moment and takes a drink from his plastic cup. 'Finally satisfied that the rumbling had stopped, she slept again, looking like a large rock to some; to others, like a small mountain.'

'Is that true?'

'It's a story.'

'Aren't you afraid the Rainbow Snake will swallow you?'

'I'm afraid the earth will swallow us all one day. I'm bushed. This bloody medicine makes me dozy.' He smiles at me before he closes his eyes. The egg is still in his hand. I watch the sheet go up and down as he breathes, until Dad comes. Susan is with him. She is wearing her white doctor's coat.

'Let's go,' she whispers. I wave goodbye to the man who got hit by the wallaby. He twists his face up again and lifts his fat watery hand.

When we get outside the ward, Susan leaves us.

'Where's she going?' I ask Dad.

'To work. Did you have a good talk with Mr M?'

'He told me about the kangaroos. Is it raining now in Akarula?'

'I expect so.'

'That's right.' And then I remember. 'There's no one left to feed the birds.' I don't want to cry, but my throat gets lumpy when I think of those birds getting thinner and thinner like Mr M.

Dad takes my hand and leads me over to the window by the reception desk. On the roof of the nearest portacabin there are a whole row of birds that look exactly the same as the pink and grey galahs in Akarula. I think about the time when Mum and Dad and me made fish shapes in the sand on Whitley Beach, and laughed until our faces hurt. I think about how I swung between the two of them: the sand trails from my shoes, our stretched-out shadows. A few of the birds take off; I watch them fly. And ever so gently, my heart bursts open.

SEREN
Well chosen words

Seren is an independent publisher with a wide-ranging list which includes poetry, fiction, biography, art, translation, criticism and history. Many of our books and authors have been on longlists and shortlists for – or won – major literary prizes, among them the Costa Award, the Jerwood Fiction Uncovered Prize, the Man Booker, the Desmond Elliott Prize, The Writers' Guild Award, Forward Prize, and TS Eliot Prize.

At the heart of our list is a good story told well or an idea or history presented interestingly or provocatively. We're international in authorship and readership though our roots are here in Wales (Seren means Star in Welsh), where we prove that writers from a small country with an intricate culture have a worldwide relevance.

Our aim is to publish work of the highest literary and artistic merit that also succeeds commercially in a competitive, fast changing environment. You can help us achieve this goal by reading more of our books – available from all good bookshops and increasingly as e-books. You can also buy them at 20% discount from our website, and get monthly updates about forthcoming titles, readings, launches and other news about Seren and the authors we publish.

www.serenbooks.com